# Sam, Moses, Matt, and Quickshaw

# Sam, Moses, Matt, and Quickshaw

≈ A Novel ≈

By Bill Donahue

Editing by Barbara Gould

iUniverse, Inc.
New York  Lincoln  Shanghai

**Sam, Moses, Matt, and Quickshaw**

Copyright © 2007 by William E. Donahue

All rights reserved. No part of this book may be used or reproduced by any means, graphic, electronic, or mechanical, including photocopying, recording, taping or by any information storage retrieval system without the written permission of the publisher except in the case of brief quotations embodied in critical articles and reviews.

iUniverse books may be ordered through booksellers or by contacting:

iUniverse
2021 Pine Lake Road, Suite 100
Lincoln, NE 68512
www.iuniverse.com
1-800-Authors (1-800-288-4677)

This is a work of fiction. All of the characters, names, incidents, organizations, and dialogue in this novel are either the products of the author's imagination or are used fictitiously.

ISBN-13: 978-0-595-41605-9 (pbk)
ISBN-13: 978-0-595-85953-5 (ebk)
ISBN-10: 0-595-41605-5 (pbk)
ISBN-10: 0-595-85953-4 (ebk)

Printed in the United States of America

I dedicate this book to Ms. Barabara Gould who inspired and encouraged the continuation and instilled the desire to write stories that could be read and enjoyed by everyone. Barbara spends many long hours giving of her freely to edit my stories and brings them to life. To my wife and children who are the backbone of allowing time and input for the stories to be completed. To everyone who encouraged along the way, and my brother Mike who spends many hours of his time sketching and bring to life the words in pictures. My thanks to Mike for his input in the cover design of the cover of this book. I hope you enjoy reading it as much as I have enjoyed writing it.

## "The Big Black Bear"

When he stood, he looked as tall as an old Oak tree
The first time I saw him, he scared the devil out of me
I'd never seen a big black bear before face to face
In this forest that I always considered my place

His hair was black as coal and his face filled with fear
I tried to scare him off, but he decided to come near
I readied myself for what I thought may be my end
I saved his life from the cliff and he became my best friend

He sees Matt, Moses and I different now than he did before
We healed his wounds that would have taken his life for sure
He was pulled to safety by those whom he meant to harm
Together they did it, nursed him to health and remained calm

When healed and ready he slowly walked away into the trees
When he was gone, in our safety, we fell to our knees
We did what we felt was right, without little or no regret
And this was one big bear that all agreed, we'd never forget

We were glad to see him go, but one day later on he came
It would have cost Matt his life, but for Matt he did the same
When he was needed somehow big bear did arrive
And because of his great strength, Matt is still alive

He came that he might repay a debt he felt he owed
And his willingness to repay, this very day he showed
Now again off into the Forrest big bear did slowly go
And if ever we'd see him again, not of us would ever know

The Big Black Bear with coal black hair
Had mighty big paws and very sharp claws
As tall as an old Oak tree, this bear is a friend to me
The Big Black Bear—give a yell, and he'll be there

# Chapter 1

## Big Black Bear

Sam slowly poked his head out of his sleeping bag. He could hear the water rushing over the rocks at the riverbed. All the sounds of nature were around him. As he listened to the birds chirping happily in the trees, he gave a silent *thank you* for being able to enjoy his job as a writer for *"Our World"* magazine. All through his career, Sam had encountered many unusual and dangerous situations. Today, high in the mountains during early spring, he mistakenly felt he was in peaceful surroundings. Little did he realize he was about to embark on his most unforgettable venture.

As Sam was enjoying the warmth of his nylon cocoon, he spotted a bald eagle in the sky. He watched in awe as the eagle glided through the air bringing its early morning catch to its nest perched high on a nearby cliff. Finally, the eagle disappeared into a fog and could no longer be seen. Sam turned over to rest for another fifteen minutes so he could enjoy the early morning symphony of nature. Suddenly, Sam felt a cold wetness about his face. It was his dog, Moses, licking him from his neck to his forehead. Sam knew this meant Moses thought it was time to get up and start the day. Instead, he moved over and hauled Moses into the sleeping bag with him. He hugged Moses tightly and said, "There's plenty of time, old boy. Relax."

Sam and Moses stayed resting for a while. Then, all of a sudden, they were stunned by the arrival of the biggest black bear either one of them had ever seen. Sam quickly darted for a tree that looked easy to climb yet high enough to escape from the bear. As Sam got ready to climb, Moses jumped on Sam's back as if to say, *Don't forget me.*

Soon they were about half way up the tree and out of reach of the big black bear. Sam held Moses tightly with one arm and gave him a kiss on the top of his head. He silently thanked Moses for not barking at the big bear. Sam could feel his own heart pounding in his chest. He was breathing heavily and wondering what would happen next. When the bear arrived at the foot of the tree, he looked up at them, growled and slowly left. Then he returned to the campsite to look for something to eat. Sam watched as the bear pawed through the containers without opening any of them. They were either too strong or too well sealed. The bear started throwing everything around. He made a mess of the campsite. Soon he was on his way. Sam kept Moses with him in the tree for a few extra minutes to make sure the bear was not coming back. When he felt they were safe again, he and Moses made their descent to the ground. Sam patted his dog's head and said, "Well, Moses, that wasn't too much fun, was it? At least we still have all our supplies."

Sam headed toward the stream to wash up and get some water for coffee. Moses followed closely behind him. As Sam neared the stream, he could see the big black bear trying to catch his breakfast. The bear didn't seem to be doing too well here, either. He had waded up to his knees and was swinging his arms madly in and out of the moving brook. Sam immediately decided that he and Moses would head back to the campsite. He could use the water he had in the canteens. He would do anything to stay clear of this new found friend.

Sam gave Moses a can of his favorite dog food, a couple of biscuits and a bowl of water. Then he started the campfire and made home fries, eggs, toast, bacon and a bubbling pot of hot coffee. Breakfast smelled so good, it made Sam realize he had never been so hungry. He got his cup, plate and some silverware. As he was ready to sit and enjoy it all, when, suddenly he heard a familiar growling in the background. He turned to see the black bear re-entering his camp. Sam ran as quickly as he could to the tree that provided a safe haven the last time. Moses was right behind him and jumped on his back. Sam watched as the bear came to the foot of the tree. It appeared to him that the bear was grinning as he looked up the tree at the two frightened figures. Then the big bear turned and slowly walked toward the campfire where the smell of a delicious breakfast had permeated the entire area. Sam looked at Moses and held him a little tighter. He was trying to convey how happy he was that they were both fairly safe. The bear was now nearing the freshly prepared breakfast. He was about to knock the pan off the fire when a gun shot rang out loudly and clearly. The black bear turned and ran as fast as he could down a path and into the woods.

At the far end of the campsite, a very tall thin man came out of the bushes. Looking up at Sam and Moses, he yelled to them, "Are you going to let this beautiful breakfast go to waste?"

Sam gave out a nervous laugh as he climbed down the tree with Moses on his back. The slender man introduced himself first, "I'm Matt, Matt Bender."

Sam extended his hand, "I'm Sam, ever grateful Sam." He shook Matt's hand and continued, "This is my companion, Moses." Moses immediately welcomed him by licking his hand.

"Come on, Matt. You certainly deserve some breakfast."

"Well now that you mention it, I don't mind if I do. Thank you."

Sam gladly shared the meal. They lingered over freshly brewed cups of coffee talking and getting to know each other. "Do you live around here, Matt?"

Matt stood up and stretched his long lanky frame of 6' 8". He ran his fingers through his natty gray and brown peppered beard that nearly reached his waist. Then Matt took his index finger and pushed his wire rim glasses in place. This is when Sam noticed that Matt's hands were twice the size of most men. Matt sat down again and folded his long legs in front of him. He finally answered, "I live about four miles from this campsite. About ten years ago, I built a small log cabin not so far from here. What brings you to my neck of the woods?"

Sam felt there was some sadness about Matt. He noticed that his clothes were shaggy and baggy. His boots and hat looked like discarded parts of a uniform from an old time army soldier. Sam decided not to ask any more questions.

"I'm on assignment to write an article for a magazine." Then he stood up and started clearing the mess they had made eating breakfast. Matt got up to his feet joined him getting everything picked up and put away.

Sam stood about 5' 10" and weighed around 185 lbs. He figured Matt did not weigh much more than he did. Standing next to Sam, Matt looked taller and thinner than he really was. Sam looked at his own beard. It only covered his neck with a few gray hairs poking out near his chin. He compared it to Matt's and asked, "How long did it take you to grow that beard?"

"Don't rightly know. It seems I've had it forever. Maybe 10 years or so."

"I only let mine grow when I am on assignment or when I go camping with Moses. I certainly envy you, 'though. It would be great not having to shave every single day."

"Suits me just fine, too. Great dog you have here."

Sam looked at Moses who stood there wagging his tail of gray and white, shaggy fur. Sam never knew what type of dog Moses was. All he knew was that Moses was the most loyal dog any man could ever have.

"You know, Sam, you and the dog are the first visitors I've seen in this area in over five years. Don't mean to frighten you, but most people 'round town stay away from here. They seem to think there's a big, wild, crazy man who lives in these mountains. They say he thinks and acts like the rest of the wild animals. Strange, but I visit here often. Haven't seen any signs of him."

When Sam saw Matt's smile, he knew it was okay to laugh with him. Sam realized then that Matt really enjoyed his time in the mountains. It became obvious to Sam that Matt did not care what others thought of him. Sam was really starting to like Matt and his laid-back sense of humor.

When they finished tidying up the campsite, Matt was the first one to sit down and continue their conversation. Sam appreciated that and he sat directly across from him. Now they were face to face. Sam no longer had to strain his neck looking up at this tall man.

Sam spotted an eagle in the sky directly above them. "Look, Matt, isn't he beautiful?"

Matt put out his arm and gave a quick whistle. The eagle came down and landed right on his forearm. Sam's mouth dropped open.

"Sam, this is Quickshaw. I found him many years ago when he was all alone and close to death. I nursed him back to health and helped him learn to fly. I guess you might say both of us have been watching over each other ever since."

All Sam could say was "Wow!" Then he asked, "Do you think it would be okay if I took a picture of, did you say his name was Quickshaw, perched on your arm?"

"I don't think that would be a good idea. I don't know how Quickshaw would react to your camera or flashbulbs."

"I guess you're right. Now that I've mentioned my camera, I remember why I am here. Since you seem to know this area so well, could you tell me where you think I could get the best pictures?"

"Tell you what. If you think you could stand a 'wild and crazy man' tagging along for a while, I'll be happy to show you what I think are the most beautiful sites."

Sam laughed and immediately started packing the camping gear. They went down a path that led along the riverbed. Sam was thankful that the bear was not around this time. He was glad that the sound of the gun frightened him. The path was extremely narrow and patchy in places. Sam followed closely behind Matt. "Looks like this path is rarely used except by wildlife and maybe you. Right, Matt?" Matt didn't bother to answer. He just looked back and gave Sam a smile.

Sam thought the path would never end. Behind him, he could hear Moses panting. He turned around and was happy to see Moses who had stopped to drink from a little pool of water. Finally, they came to where the path seemed to head straight up to the clouds. Sam was relieved until he saw that the next portion of the path included a climb over rocks that were slippery. Sam saw how easily Matt made the climb. He was hoping he could do the same. He could not. About half way, he asked "Do you think we could take a quick break?"

Matt turned around and gave Sam a knowing smile. "Sure thing."

They each took a little drink of water and chatted about the area for a few minutes. Then they began the rest of their journey. Sam helped himself to several of the berries and fruits along the path. When they finally came to a flat spot, they walked into a small clearing just as the sun began to fade. Matt said "This is as far as we should go for the night." Sam happily nodded in agreement.

As they set up camp, they could hear the many beautiful sounds of nature all around them once more. The dark blue sky began to fill with bright sparkling stars.

After the evening meal and before going to bed, Sam asked "Matt, what brought you to this area and kept you here for such a long time?"

Sam watched as Matt was deciding whether or not to share his story. After a little deliberation, he began, "I was a farmer for many years. I guess I was lucky enough to own about a hundred and seventy five acres of great farmland. I really enjoyed my life, back then. Guess I never minded hard work. Of course, you must know by now how much I love the outdoors."

Sam nodded and smiled. He waited to see if Matt would continue.

"I had a beautiful wife and two children, a boy and a girl. Life was great and I was content knowing I had everything in life I wanted."

Then Matt's voice changed. His face took on a serious far-away look. "One day, when I was in town buying supplies, an unexpected storm hit our whole town. It left me stranded. The waters were so high I couldn't travel back home. The winds were blowing trees and debris all over the place. People in town had to leave their homes and stay in nearby shelters. There were no phones or any other means of communication in or out of town. That horrible storm lasted for three and a half days. When it was finally over, it had ruined most of the town. It was a week before I could head back home."

Matt stopped, took a hard swallow and continued, "When I finally got back to where my farm was, everything was gone. The only thing I could see was a new lake. My home and farm were completely under water.

Everything was under water. There were no signs of life anywhere. Volunteers helped me search the entire perimeter of the lake for days. We never found any signs of my wife or children. I didn't know where to go or what to do. The lake never dried up. All I remember is that I just wanted to die and blame everything on God. For a long time, I tried in vain to see if my wife and children had sought shelter somewhere. I searched for two whole years and then I just had to stop. I realized I was living on false hopes. Then, I went to work for a paper factory in a nearby town. As the days passed, I became frustrated from being confined in a building with odors that were making me sick."

Matt stopped and looked at Sam, "Have you had enough of my sad story, Sam?"

"No, please, continue."

"Okay, if you're sure you want to hear it. One day, I took the little money I had managed to save and decided to leave and go somewhere, anywhere. I put all my belongings in a knapsack and left with a few dollars in my pocket. I journeyed as far as I could until I guess I just collapsed from exhaustion. When I awoke the next morning, I decided this was where I would make my new home. I fell in love with the life I found here among the hills and the trees. Every day I thank God for such beautiful land. I also ask his forgiveness for some of the blame I put on him when I lost everything. Maybe I am a little crazy and wild. What do you think, Sam?"

Sam felt empathy for Matt's misfortune but was happy that he was able to find some peace. "I'm sorry about the loss of your family and farm, Matt."

"Thank you."

"I'm glad the rest of your life brought you here. Moses and I are proud to know you. Who knows what might have happened to us if you had not come by when you did? You probably saved our lives."

Matt grinned, but said nothing. Moses snuggled closer to Sam and was allowed to share the sleeping bag for the night. The evening was quiet and beautiful. The sounds were similar to an orchestra being led by God himself. It was a great night for sleeping and all awoke the next day bright and cheery. They felt well rested, hungry and eager to continue their trek. Sam and Matt quietly ate a hardy breakfast. They were soon on their way again. As they were getting near the top of the path, they could see over the tops of the trees. Sam was beginning to understand why Matt was leading him to this spot. He could tell that the scenery would be breathtaking just from the little bit he could see now. He couldn't wait to get to the top. He had a new burst of energy. Soon he was at Matt's side. Then he passed him. Moses kept up the pace and stayed at Sam's heels.

As he passed Matt, Sam could faintly hear "I'm glad you like it, Sam."

By late morning, they arrived at the very top of the mountain. They dropped their backpacks and gear. They sat back in awe to enjoy the unbelievably gorgeous view. Sam started to jot down a few notes. "Directly before me are varied trees displaying the most beautiful array of colors against the background of a cloudless sky?"

It wasn't long before Quickshaw arrived. He stayed as silent as the others and appeared to be enjoying the view. Then, he let out a loud screech. Matt turned around just in time to see the big black bear come charging out of the bushes. Matt shouted, "Sam. Look out!"

Sam leaped to his feet. He could see the black bear heading straight for him. His heart was beating so fast, he thought it was going to burst. Somehow he was able to jump out of the way causing the big black bear to slip and fall over the edge of the cliff.

"Good heavens, Sam, where did you learn to jump like that? Don't tell me you were part of a circus group before you took up writing."

Sam was too frightened to respond. Matt helped him to his feet. Moses contributed by licking Sam's hand. Sam wiped his forehead and said,"Phew! That was too close for comfort!"

Then, after calming down for a while, Sam suggested they start preparing lunch. Sam thought he could hear something. "Hey, Matt, can you hear that noise? It sounds like crying or moaning."

"Yeah, I do hear something. Let's look around to see what or who it is."

They searched everywhere, but found nothing. Suddenly, Moses was barking and looking down the edge of the cliff. Sam and Matt went over to Moses to see what was bothering him. They saw that the big black bear had landed on a ledge about a third of the way down on the side of the cliff. Matt asked, "Sam do you have any rope?"

"Sure I do, but what do you plan on doing with it?"

"Well, we just might be able to save the bear. That is, if we can get to him."

Sam looked at Matt as if he were losing his mind. "Save the bear! Why would you want to save that bear?"

"I just can't stand by and watch any animal die that way. He would surely starve to death. I just can't let that happen without trying to save him."

Sam had mixed emotions. He did not want to see the bear suffer, but he also did not want to give the bear another attempt on his life, either. Deep in his heart, he knew Matt was right. He went to get the rope and passed it to Matt. Matt passed him one end and held on to the other.

Sam tied one end of the rope to a very large tree while Matt tied the other end around his own waist. Sam watched as Matt made his way down the cliff. Matt positioned himself just to the right of the big black bear. Sam thought he could see the bear becoming docile and ready to accept some help. Actually, the bear was semi-conscious and in a lot of pain. Matt whispered gently to the bear "I'll be right back." Sam wondered if Matt thought the bear could understand him. Then he remembered all the conversations he has had with Moses.

Matt made his way to the top of the cliff. "Well, Sam, any suggestions on how we can get the bear up here where he'll be safe?"

They spent a long time going over many ideas. It seemed as if nothing was going to work. Finally, they decided to make a sling out of some extra clothes Sam had brought with him. They gathered some small, but strong, branches and put it all together. Sam saw how anxious Matt was to attempt the rescue. Sam kept hoping they were doing the right thing.

"Okay, Sam. It seems like this is our only chance to save him. I think we made a sturdy sling. Let's hope it will do the trick."

Once everything was prepared and their plan was in place, they tied the rope around the sling and tossed it over the cliff. Matt made his way down the rope. When he arrived near the bear, he could see that the bear was still drowsy. Gently, and with very slow movements, he made his way to the bear's side. He was able to place the sling flat behind the bear. Although it took all the strength Matt could muster, and a little bit of movement from the bear, he managed to get the bear positioned in the center of the sling. Then Matt made his way up the rope to the top of the cliff. With long strong branches, Matt and Sam were able to start lifting the bear up a little at a time. They locked the rope in place every once in a while in order to catch their breath. They would take a quick sip of water and hope to regain their strength. It took them almost three hours to raise the bear to safety and have him on flat ground where they could get a better look at him. They looked at each other. Sam spoke first, "He sure is a big one! I cannot deny that he still frightens me."

"As well he should." said Matt, "We have to take some precautions here and right now."

They decided to tie his arms and legs while they examined him. They had to shave back many parts of his fur to treat most of the wounds. They spent almost two and one half hours finding all the bruises he had from his fall. He was beginning to awake so they slowly and very carefully fed him some corn bread and fresh water. Night was beginning to fall. They left the bear tied up for the night, just to be on the safe side. They would discuss a way to safely free him in the morning. The evening was quiet and without any problems. The bear seemed to rest and was able to sleep even though he must have been in a lot of pain and very uncomfortable.

The morning sun was burning Sam's face. He opened his eyes and saw Moses quietly staring at the bear. Sam wondered if Moses was up all night checking on this huge animal. Sam felt that he and Moses had every reason to fear this bear.

"Okay, Sam. Let's go over our plan, one more time. We'll give the bear some corn bread and water. Then you take Moses up the tree and get ready to help me join you as soon as I free the bear. Got it?"

"We got it."

All went exactly as planned. As the bear slowly walked away, he looked back at his brave rescuers sitting in the tree. Sam asked Matt, "Am I dreaming or does that bear understand what we did for him?"

"You know, I think he does. He seemed as if he was trying to thank us. I could have sworn I saw a grin on his face."

"Yeah, me too. What an experience and I can't ever write about it. Who would believe me?"

Then Sam remembered his first few encounters with the bear. "Do you suppose he will return and put us in danger again? Maybe it was a mistake to help him and set him free?"

"No, Sam, we did the right thing. Now, relax. Let's eat our breakfast and then you can try to find something worth photographing. I don't know about you, but I'm as hungry as a bear."

Sam didn't find any humor in Matt's statement. "Okay, let's get breakfast started."

After satisfying his appetite, Sam took out his photography equipment. He wanted Matt and Moses to stand near the cliff so he could capture the beautiful background behind them. Neither seemed interested and went off in their own direction. Sam began taking pictures. They spent the next few days in an area of about a mile square finding plants, trees, flowers, berries and fruit. The mountains against the sky line. The clouds that seemed to sit atop the mountains. It was all just overwhelming. Picture after picture produced more excitement with each click of the camera. As many times as Sam tried to get Matt and Moses to pose, he could not. They would go in another direction. Sam managed to get them unexpectedly that evening when they seemed mesmerized by the crackling campfire. Sam was pleased with himself. He felt that picture would be better and more natural than one where they had to pose, anyway.

Sam and Matt had been together almost a month before Sam realized how much time had passed. During this time, Sam and Matt had built quite a relationship. Moses and Quickshaw seemed to be getting along quite well, also. One day, Matt said "My cabin is within four or five miles from here. Why don't we head in that direction?"

"Sounds like a plan to me."

They arrived at the cabin to find everything intact; nothing had been disturbed. Sam knew Matt must re-live his nightmarish experience of ten years ago every time he comes home. Sam watched as Matt put a bowl of water down for Moses. He pulled up a couple of chairs. "Come on Sam. I think we deserve to rest." He filled two glasses with fresh spring water and then he and Sam just sat back and relaxed.

Sam sat there quietly reflecting on the events of the past few months. He knew he would never have found such beautiful treasures of nature without Matt's help and knowledge of the hills. He would always be grateful to Matt for having rescued him and Moses. He hoped he and Matt would remain friends for a long time. Sam could not have realized what would soon happen to his new friend, Matt.

They spent much time around the cabin over the next couple of weeks. They became used to sleeping in beds again. The cabin was small and equipped with only the bare necessities. There were homemade candles for light that Matt had learned to make himself. There was a fireplace for heating and cooking, a table with two chairs, and a bunk bed. The floor was still dirt and the windows were of plastic sheeting. However, the house was very dry and as clean as it could be.

When Matt first came to the hills, he started carving wooden objects as a means of relaxation. He practiced and practiced until he had mastered the art. When he felt he was good enough, he carved, from memory, a small statue of his wife and two children. He kept the statue on a wooden mantle over the fireplace. He smiled as he talked about them and the plans they once had. Matt began to carve statues of both Sam and Moses standing side by side on a mountain. He did his best to make it look as lifelike as possible. He spent a lot of time working on it.

When morning came, Sam was awakened by the sound of a tree being chopped in the distance. He jumped out of bed, had a quick bite to eat and ran off to see what Matt was up to so early in the morning. When he arrived, he saw that Matt was almost through the tree. Matt stopped when he saw Sam. "You know, Sam, I have been after this tree for a long time."

"Why?" Sam asked.

"Do you know there is enough wood in this one tree for an entire winter?"

Sam chuckled and as he walked away and said, "Probably. See you in three days or so. That's a mighty big tree!"

Matt went back to work as Sam left and laughed out loud with every swing of the axe.

Sam didn't get very far when he heard Matt holler, "Timber!" He also heard Matt holler again, "Oh, no!"

As Sam turned to watch, he could see the falling tree was heading right for Matt. There was nothing he could do. The tree was too big and Matt was too far away. Sam felt helpless and just knelt down, praying the tree would miss his new friend.

The tree finally landed and Sam began yelling, "Matt, Matt, are you okay? Matt, Matt, where are you?" There was no answer. All Sam could hear was dead silence.

Sam started running toward the fallen tree. Moses had found Matt first. He tried licking Matt's face, but received no response whatsoever. Matt was unconscious. He was pinned under the tree about fifteen feet from the top. Sam ran to his side and found that he was still alive. He tried to pull him free. It was no use. One of Matt's legs was pinned too tightly under the tree. Sam quickly ran to the cabin to get water and rags. When he returned, Matt was still unconscious.

Quickshaw flew down to the area and stayed close to Matt. Sam took the rags and soaked them in the cool spring water. Then he began to wipe Matt's forehead. He softly asked, "Matt, can you hear me?"

Matt opened his eyes and tried to say something a few times, but he could not. He just kept losing consciousness. Sam continued to wipe the cool water on Matt's forehead. Finally, after some time, Matt was able to open his eyes and keep them opened. He grinned and said, "I came to get the tree, but the tree got me"

"Take it easy, Matt. You're still pinned under it. I don't know how and I don't know when, but I can assure you that somehow, someway, I will get you free. You can depend on that!"

Moses ran off and came back with a small branch in his mouth. Sam laughed and thanked his faithful friend for trying to be of some help. Sam spent the next few hours just trying to keep Matt relaxed and cool. At least three hours had passed before Sam felt he could leave Matt's side to find something he could use to help free him.

Sam looked for hours and thought of many different ways to move the tree. However, none of them was about to work. He was just about ready to go and try to find help when he heard a growling noise behind him. It sounded like a very large bear. He turned and quickly bent to pick up the biggest branch he could find to protect his friend, Matt. He stood straight and firm holding the stick high in the air. The bear didn't seem to be very aggressive. Then Moses slowly started walking toward the bear. Sam called, "Moses, come back!"

Moses, ignoring Sam's command, continued moving closer to the bear. Moses was now side by side with the bear. Sam was baffled. To him, it appeared they were talking to each other. The bear got down on all fours and came slowly toward the tree. As he moved in closer, Sam could see he was exactly like the big black bear that had fallen over the cliff. He wondered if this could possibly be the same one. The bear and Moses were now near the tree just a few feet from where Matt was pinned under it. Suddenly, Sam could see that the bear was getting ready to lift the tree. Sam quickly positioned himself closer to Matt and held him by the shoulders. The big black bear had his arms under the tree. With a great groan, he lifted the tree just high enough for Sam to pull Matt free. The bear then grabbed Matt's long, limp body and, following Moses' lead, carried him back to the cabin. He placed him gently on a table outside. Then, Sam immediately ripped back the leg of Matt's pants to expose his damaged limb. The leg was open and bleeding in a number of places. It did not look good. Sam went into the cabin to get some medical supplies. He silently prayed that he would be able to save Matt's leg.

The big black bear, Quickshaw and Moses stood by quietly just watching and waiting. Sam was able to find everything he needed. He started by cleaning off all the blood. Then he applied medication to all the wounded areas. He bandaged Matt's leg, and told him, "Just lie back and try to get some rest."

Matt did as he was told. He didn't really have too much to say in the matter. Sam walked over to the big black bear and very gently said "Thank you." The big black bear stood up on his two hind legs and gave a diminished growl. Sam took that to mean "You're welcome." Then the big black bear turned and headed into the woods behind them.

Quickshaw flew to his nest high on the mountain. In just moments, he had disappeared behind the tall trees. Moses crawled over near the table and found a soft spot on the grass where he could stay until Matt was through resting. Matt rested for about six hours. He finally awoke just as the sun was setting. Sam got him some water and held the glass to make it easier for him to drink. Sam wiped Matt's forehead again and checked the bandages. Moses started licking his face. Sam looked at his friend and said with all honesty, "It's good to have you back. Matt."

"Thanks, Sam. I am feeling better. You know, it's odd. My leg doesn't hurt as much anymore. What did you do, cut if off?"

Sam laughed. "Well, I guess your sense of humor has returned. I suppose you've also regained your appetite. I'll start supper. Think you can stay out of trouble that long?"

"Suppose I could try."

When they were finished eating, Sam helped Matt into the house and to his bed. This was no easy task. Matt was so much taller than Sam. He had to put one of his big hands on the top of Sam's head just to keep from falling. Sam did not mind. All that concerned him was that Matt could get to bed and have a good night's rest.

The next morning, Sam was awakened by Moses who was barking at something in the yard. Sam came to the top of the porch stairs and could not believe what he saw. There stood the big black bear with a paw full of fish. Sam wondered if he was dreaming. He was overwhelmed wondering how a wild creature could actually be concerned. He found it difficult to understand how the bear knew they would not be able to get out and catch breakfast now that Matt was hurt. Sam stood there frozen in disbelief. The bear laid the fish on the outside table and again gave a diminished soft growl before he turned and disappeared into the woods. He did this every day for a week and a half. Then one morning, he saw that Matt was on his feet again. That was the last time he came.

Matt's leg healed faster than Sam had expected. Apparently the wounds were not as bad as they looked. He was up and about in just one month.

One day, when Matt was kneeling beside the large tree that had fallen on him, Sam asked, "Why this tree?"

Matt explained, "This tree, Sam, can supply a lot of firewood, probably enough for an entire season. The inside is the best wood anywhere for carving. The core of the tree is soft enough to work, but hard enough to withstand time. It holds the coats of varnish I use better than any other wood I have ever seen. Actually, all the furniture in the house was made from the same type of tree. I cut one down when I first came to this area. I guess the main reason is that the wood is amazingly easy to use, yet it is extremely strong."

Matt found out how easy the wood was to carve when he created his first piece of furniture. He used a strip he had leftover after making the furniture to make his very first carving.

"Guess what my first carving was." Matt asked. "Oh, I don't know, maybe a deer?" Was Sam's reply. Would you believe it was a big black bear?"

Sam laughed. "You must have ESP."

The big black bear did not return. Sam and Matt knew they may never see him again. They did not realize they were about to lose another loved one.

# Chapter 2

## The Search for Moses

It was fairly quiet. The aroma of fresh coffee brewing on the campfire in the front yard was beckoning Sam to come back for another cup. Sam was just standing there listening to the birds merrily singing and chirping. He could also hear the morning's gentle breeze as it rustled through the trees. It was a beautiful morning. "Come on, Sam. We've got to finish packing if you want to get going. You're the one who wants to take some fancy pictures. Let's go!"

Sam knew Matt was right. An early start was what they needed. "Alright, alright, I'm coming."

Sam's friendship with Matt grew stronger every day. He really enjoyed the time they were spending together. Having such a close friendship was a new experience for him. He had never taken the time to build any strong friendships before. He was always too busy with work or with Moses. He knew the day would come when he would have to go back to the office and complete his assignment. The pictures were going to make the article much better than he had expected. He was excited about that, but reluctant about leaving Matt and his 'home away from home'.

Moses watched as the two of them were trying to find everything they were going to need. Moses became bored and went outside. He started playing with a twig. He tossed it up and then tried to catch it. Once he caught it, he rolled it back and forth as if it were alive and some sort of playmate. He continued to play until Sam and Matt were ready to leave. They secured the house and started their new journey. For about a mile, the path was great. It was almost flat and free of debris. This made it easier for them to walk and talk. They took the time to really see and enjoy everything around them. Matt kept asking Sam, "Have you ever seen anything so beautiful in all your life?"

Sam always responded with, "Wow. This is beautiful!" It was. It was far more beautiful than anything he had ever seen. Moses seemed happy with everything as well.

Soon, the path was not so noticeable. Matt had to take the lead. They had to walk in single file. They stopped many times to cut branches and thick brush. This really took time. They didn't get as far as they had planned for the first day. They were able to find a suitable place to make camp for the night. They gathered wood and made a fire. Sam was a little tired. "Let's just sit back and catch our breath before we warm up the vegetable soup."

"Sounds like a plan to me." Matt said as he stretched his long frame before sitting down.

There was no need to close the sleeping bags that night. It was warm and comfortable. The moon was full and the night was quiet. The crackling of the burning wood was all that broke the silence. Later that evening, wolves could be heard howling in the distance. Moses perked up, listened for a short while and then went back to sleep totally exhausted from the day's journey.

Morning brought a cooler, mistier daybreak. Sam and Matt started the fire and the coffee. Then they packed everything carefully to keep out any dampness. They left to get an early start. They were hoping to make up some of the time they lost yesterday. The path was no easier than it had been the day before. The dampness made it tougher to get good footing. They were slowed down to a snail's pace.

It started to rain quite heavily around noontime. They were literally getting soaked. Moses just stood still and barked as loudly as he could.

Sam put his hand under Moses' neck and asked "What do you want? I can't stop the rain, you know."

Moses kept on barking. Finally, Sam realized that Moses wanted them to follow him. Moses led them to a cave not too far away. They carefully went inside where the rain could not reach them. Once inside they put down all their gear as soon as they found a dry place to lay it. They took a few minutes to search inside the cave to make certain they weren't taking an animal's home. They did not need to put themselves in that kind of danger.

Sam and Matt got some branches and built a small fire inside the cave to help eliminate the dampness. The heavy rain continued and kept them confined for days. They used this time to dry everything so it would be in tip-top shape when they were able to leave again. Moses didn't seem to mind or become too restless. He just laid back and enjoyed the extra rest. He was now going on ten years old and was certainly not considered a 'spring chicken' anymore.

Finally, one morning, they awoke to something different. It was the welcomed rays from the sun shining through the entrance of the cave.

Sam sat up, "Listen, Matt. We can hear the birds chirping again".

Matt and Sam approached the entrance and then stood in disbelief. There, before them, was one of the most beautiful rainbows. It wasn't just a rainbow with the normal few colors. It was a rainbow with every possible color imaginable. Each color had its own brilliance blended into the next. All the colors complimented each other and made each and every color more beautiful. The soft blue of the cloudless sky formed the background and made the rainbow extraordinary. They were speechless and didn't care if they ever left that spot. As far as they were concerned, this moment could last forever. Sam quickly fetched his camera and was able to capture the extraordinary beauty of the rainbow before it disappeared. Soon it was replaced by gentle white-fluffy clouds rolling along as if seeking a journey of their own. Each cloud seemed to have its own form.

"Look," Sam said "do you remember when you were younger and you thought you could see just about anything in those clouds?"

"Younger? I still do it. Sometimes I think I see dragons, fish, dinosaurs, dogs, cats, lots of different things. I'll bet you still do it, too. Who are you kidding?"

Sam smiled and said "Let's get going. We have to make up a lot of time. We are at least three days behind schedule, right?"

Matt nodded. "I'll make a quick campfire and get the coffee started. I'll give Moses some biscuits and you can start the packing. Then we can get going again."

They were reinvigorated after all that rest and were able to move right along in spite of the heavy brush. By noon, they had really covered quite a distance. They took a short break near a waterfall that just seemed to make the spot a great place to rest.

Matt took Sam to a nearby tree and told him this tree was the same type as the one that had fallen on him. Matt told Sam that it was just a young tree, but when the day came that he needed his next one, he'd know where to find it.

"Try to plan the drop a little better the next time." Sam could not resist chiding him. Matt laughed and said "You can count on it."

Sam did not have to remind Matt that he had been very lucky; they both knew that. Moses had gone to the river and was playing in the water when Sam hollered to him and told him they were ready to go. Moses came right away and they continued their trek. Before long, they came to a beautiful valley. It was surrounded by very high hills and a triple waterfall at the far end. They cleared a path as they made their way down to the center of the valley. Moses ran ahead to play in the meadow that was filled with every type of flower one could imagine. All the flowers were in full bloom. There were apple trees, orange trees, cherry trees, blackberry bushes, blueberry bushes and raspberry bushes. There was also at least an acre of strawberry plants. Sam and Matt made their way to the foot of the waterfall. It certainly looked big from their vantage point. It seemed like it just kept going up and about to touch the sky.

At the foot of the waterfall, was a beautiful basin of which one side had a soft sandy beach. Sam looked at Matt. "Shall we do it?"

"Why not?"

They took their shoes off, walked in the sand and waded in the shallow water. Later, they lay on a blanket in the sand.

"If there is a heaven, we must have found it."

Matt agreed. "This has to be the most peaceful place I have ever found." They set up camp and decided this would be where Sam would take his pictures. Sam had a long hard time of deciding which angle he should take on the waterfall. Every time he set up, out of the corner of his eye he felt he could see a more perfect angle. There was so much beauty, and he knew the sad part was that the camera, because of limited scope would never capture the one thing that made it so beautiful, it's vastness. He was able to capture Matt and Moses in a couple of pictures without them knowing it. His favorite was when he captured Quickshaw gliding down over the waterfall with his own breakfast in his mouth. He spent the day with them and seemed to enjoy each of them enjoying what he saw everyday.

As the sun went down, the campfire flickered in the night, and shone against the waterfall making it look like a giant mural painted by the hand of God himself. Sam found just the right spot. He set up his camera equipment and experimented with many different lenses to see which ones would best capture the beauty before him. They were just settling back with coffee and a good book when Quickshaw arrived once more at the camp as if he wanted to say goodnight to everyone. He landed on a small branch next to Matt and looked quite comfortable with the surroundings. It appeared to Sam that Quickshaw knew this place very well. Moses crept nearer to Quickshaw. Moses looked at him and welcomed him with a simple tilt and twist of his head. They had become as close as Sam and Matt.

The night was still. The falling water and the flickering campfire served as soft music for the evening. The stars seem to shine even brighter than usual against the dark sky. Sam and Matt must have counted at least ten 'shooting stars' each. Every time they spotted one fall, they would gasp with excitement and Moses would gently whine. The night was so beautiful Sam and Matt did not want to sleep too soon.

Sam commented to Matt, "You know, it's a shame that no one has been able to invent a camera that can truly capture all this beauty the way we see it with our own eyes. It really is the vastness as during the day of everything together that makes it more beautiful. It's the blending of each individual piece of splendor that creates the majestic beauty. No one would ever capture all this."

"Thank God they can't," Matt stated "because then it would be taken for granted and no one would venture to experience it personally."

Sam agreed and they finally all fell asleep.

Their sleep was so deep and so sound that neither awoke until nine thirty the next morning. Before long, the aroma of coffee and corned beef hash filled the air. Moses was looking for his morning meal. Sam quickly got a bowl of water and took care of Moses before they sat down to eat. During breakfast, they decided they would scout around to see what hidden, undiscovered wonders they could find. As they came along the side of the waterfall, they saw what looked like an entrance to a cave. They lit a lantern and cautiously entered. Once inside, they found there was no need for the lantern. The cave was self lit by beautifully colored crystals of all different shades. Each sparkled with its own beauty and ray of light. The walls were surrounded by mini waterfalls everywhere. They flowed into the same spring that ran underground to the basin at the bottom of the large waterfall. The walls were shining as if they were lined in gold that had streaks of silver running through it. As they approached the far corner of the cave, they noticed windows that exposed the falls just in front of them. They turned to the right. They could see what looked like steps going up along the side of the walls. Sam looked at Matt, "We've come this far. We might as well climb them."

"I'd be disappointed in you if we didn't."

After going up a few stairs, they came to a platform where the stairs would stop and begin again in just a short distance. They finally reached one level where they found a room with a table and chairs, benches and something similar to bunk beds. There were no cobwebs in the room, yet it looked as if it had been years since anyone had been there. There were bowls and cups, cooking pots and eating utensils. Everything was there to set up housekeeping. They found some tablets with some very strange writing on them. Nothing appeared to be in any recognizable language.

Sam teased Matt. "Think you can figure out what these say?"

"Don't look at me. I'm just a farmer, remember? You're the scholar. You read them to me."

"Sure Matt, right after I take these pictures."

Sam quickly photographed everything. They left without disturbing a thing.

They went back into the cave area and to the next flight of stairs. The stairwell rounded consistently with the walls of the cave. At the next level, they discovered a large room filled with what looked like benches. It appeared there were enough places to seat one hundred people. There were drawings and writings all over the walls and something similar to a pulpit at the front of the room. Sam took more pictures and then sat quietly for a few moments. He hollered to Moses to follow him out to the cave again.

As they climbed the next flight of stairs, they looked down through the center of all the stairways and were able to see the cave in its entirety. It was unbelievably breathtaking. They continued toward the top of the stairs where they thought they could see daylight. In a few moments, they were walking through another entrance that led them outside. They found themselves at the top of a small mountain with a great lake that sparkled and glittered from the bright yellow and red sunshine. They walked to the edge of the lake and could see the waterfall from the top. It looked like a set of giant steps with water running over them. They could see the campsite far below them. It looked tiny from this high perspective. Climbing a mountain this size, by trails, should have been exhausting. However, they were climbing on the inside where it was cool. They reached the top with little effort. They sat on the bank of the lake and were joined by Quickshaw. Sam felt they were now in his territory.

As he just sat and took it all in, Sam suddenly realized Moses was no longer with them. Sam rose to his feet but, as far as he could see, Moses was nowhere in the entire area. He began to holler his name. There was no response. He whistled loudly and called his name again and again. Still, there was no response. There was nothing. It wasn't like Moses to be out of Sam's sight. Sam was very concerned. Sam and Matt decided to scout the area. Matt commanded Quickshaw "Go find Moses."

They spent the entire day looking in and out of bushes, caves and rock formations. They even looked in a few old, rotted out, hollow logs lying on the ground. Moses was nowhere to be found. They met at the entrance to the cave. Then it dawned on them that he may be in the cave. They hadn't thought of that.

Sam and Matt spent the next three hours searching every inch of the cave from top to bottom. They could not believe how vast it was inside the cave. Finally they decided that it was clear. Moses was not there. They would have to decide on a plan to search the area around the cave. It was getting dark and they were going to have to turn in for the night. They did not extinguish their high fire. They wanted to be certain that Moses could see it even from a level above the cave.

At the first sign of light, they were both up and ready to start a fresh search. A heavy drizzle was making the ground damp. They decided that they should stay together and sweep one area at a time. They returned to the entrance of the cave. They looked around for signs that could tell which direction Moses might have taken. There were no signs anywhere. They decided to follow along a faint clearing that may have been used for a path many years ago.

After several hours, they came to an open area. There were signs and remnants of a small group of grass huts. There were stones that must have been used for fireplaces and chimneys. There were many items all over the area suggesting that it was once inhabited.

Matt and Sam were there for a while checking to see if this was where Moses could have spent the night. There were no signs to indicate he had. They entered one of the huts that still had some shape to it.

As they entered, they saw a wall with a set of old shelves that looked like they were about to fall apart. Matt immediately went to touch one of the shelves to see what kind of wood was used. Just as he put one of his large hands on the wall and was reaching for the shelf with other, the wall moved.

"Am I seeing things, Sam, or did this wall just move?"

"It did, Matt. It really did." Sam's voice almost cracked with excitement.

They made some small torches. They had to move the old shelves to make room for them to squeeze into the opening. As they made their way through, each of them found a couple of books that looked like they were still readable. They tucked them under their arms and continued on. Once inside, they could see it was another cave. Unlike the other cave, it was not self lit. Matt extinguished his torch. Sam used his to lead the way along a very rough wall. The walls were bare except for a lot of dampness. The sand on the floor was quite cold. They made their way to a very large room that had stone benches in it. When Sam saw all the torches around the wall, he used his to light them. In minutes the room was as bright as could be. Sam and Matt just looked at each other.

"How could someone build such a place so long ago? What kind of tools did they have then?" Sam did not expect or receive any answers from Matt.

Now that they had more light, they could see that there were also some large chairs at the front of the room facing the benches. As tall as Matt was, when he sat in one of the big chairs, he looked very small. It appeared the room had been built especially for the leaders of the groups, whoever they were. It was quite an interesting room even though it was very plain. The walls had built-in shelves and some shapes not known to either Sam or Matt. They left the torches burning and headed down one of three hallways. Each hallway went in different directions off the main room. They hadn't walked very far when they came to a room with a very heavy stone door. It took all the strength both of them could muster to open that door. Once it was opened wide enough, they entered to find bones and sculls all over the room.

"Look" Matt said with a slight frown "the door latch will only allow the door to open from the outside. This must have been some type of jail cell."

Sam looked around. There were no signs of chains or irons anywhere. "They must have been thrown in here and left to die of starvation. What a way to go!"

They just looked at each other with disgust and pity written on their faces.

They could not get out of there quickly enough. They were only able to go back to the big room. They stopped long enough to see what the books were about that they had picked up back at the entrance. They could make out that two of them were on stone building and rock formation. Still another was on foods and cooking means, and making of utensils, etc. "Matt!" Exclaimed Sam as he opened the fourth book. "Look at this. It looks like a book of generations of the people who once lived here and in the surrounding area." They read on and tried to get as much out of it as possible. Toward the end of the book it looked as if someone were writing about a big storm that was going on as he was writing. About heavy rains, falling rocks, and the flooding of the caves. He continued on to say it didn't look like any of them may survive whatever it was, that was going on. There must have been people here at one time and it was quite clear that the writer was right, none of them had survived.

They decided to try another hallway still hoping to find Moses. The hall was very long. Before Sam's torch ran down, they used it to ignite Matt's again. As they walked a little farther, they could see an opening in the distance. When they reached the opening, they had daylight all around them. They could see what once had been a great garden surrounded by stone walls at least twenty feet in height. These stones were stacked beautifully. They must have been made by some type of human.

The sun was very high and able to fill the entire area with beautiful sunlight. Earlier in the day, it would have been shaded. Two hours from now, it would be shaded again. It seemed as though it was designed to allow just so much sun to come in for the day. They must have felt that, if the walls were shorter, whatever they were growing would receive too much sun. Sam and Matt looked around for a telltale sign of what might have been grown here. They found nothing. There was however, what looked like a lot of small caves built into the walls with small openings as if doors, or windows, etc.

Suddenly, they could hear an eagle. They looked to the top of the wall and they saw Quickshaw sitting and calling to them. They hollered up and asked if he had seen Moses anywhere. They surmised he was telling them he had not seen him. After seeing that Sam and Matt had not found Moses either, Quickshaw flew off to continue his search. Matt and Sam returned and headed down the rest of the old path. They had not gone very far when Sam spotted what looked like the entrance to another cave. This one was situated just below a small cliff. Once they removed the debris, they were able to find two torches near the entrance. They lit one and took the other along as a back-up. Not too long after they entered the cave, they found it also had a split. This cave was covered with more cobwebs than the any of the others they had searched. Neither of them could understand why. With all the searching they had done and the areas they had covered, they found no signs that any living thing had been around these secluded areas for many, many years. Sam wondered if Moses would be the exception. He tried to fight the sadness he was feeling. As he walked along he continued to call out for his missing friend, Moses.

They had walked some distance before finding it to be a dead end. As they turned to go back, Sam lost his footing and fell against a wall. The wall began to move. Matt quickly grabbed on to Sam to keep him from disappearing. Sam could feel the coldness of the wall as his back hit it. He fell to the ground. Matt had a hold on Sam's sleeve and did not let go until, he, too, was on the ground. "You okay, Sam?"

"Yes, I'm alright. Thanks."

Once they were both on their feet, they inspected the wall until they learned how to make it move. It opened into a very large room. They were hesitant to enter for fear that they may not know how to leave. They wedged a few large rocks between the door and the wall. When they were sure the rocks would keep the door open, they carefully entered the room. They found what looked like some type of bedroom. There were shelves made of long straight slabs of rock, a large rock carved to look like a chair and another very large slab rock that resembled a bed. There were a few smaller rock formations that could have been used for small night stands or tables for tiny items. There was nothing to indicate it may have been a prison or cell of some type, because there were no signs of bones anywhere in the room.

Sam made his way to the large slab bed and jokingly said, "Ah, just what I need, a little rest." When his hand hit the part of the bed that looked like a pillow, it caused a portion of the floor below the bed to open.

He and Matt quickly grabbed some rocks to use to try to keep it opened. They looked down the opening, but they could not see anything. It was much too deep and dark. The torches did not shed enough light to help. They dropped a few stones and listened to see how long it would take before they heard them hit bottom. Matt estimated that it might be about ten to twelve feet deep.

Matt said, "I think we can manage this. Are you willing to try?"

Sam replied, "We've come this far. I can't give up now. Let's go."

Matt took Sam by the hands and lowered him into the hole. When Matt heard Sam say he was standing on flat ground he carefully passed him the torch. Then Matt held on to one edge of the hole and dropped himself, feet first, next to Sam. As they looked around, they could see it was another very large room with only the opening above them for an exit. They checked the walls for any hidden passages. They were all solid and none of them showed any movement. Again, they found no sign of Moses. They had to leave. Matt stood on Sam's shoulders and was back in the room in just minutes. Then he helped lift Sam. They removed the rocks and watched as the opening closed slowly and quietly. They continued walking very carefully, looking at every turn for an opening that might lead them to Moses. Suddenly, the cave became a very large room, bigger than they had seen so far. Before them, appearing out of nowhere was what looked like a thirty or forty foot high waterfall. At the base of the waterfall was a pond of at least fifty feet in diameter. It had a very high, crystal-clear water fountain that squirted straight up and nearly touched a fifty or sixty foot high ceiling. Many different types of green, orange, red and yellow ivy vines covered at least twenty feet on both sides of the wall space of this spectacular, foamy-white waterfall. Around the edges of the pond were many beautiful, yet drab bushes. From the far corner, a ray of sunlight was coming in from the high side of the wall. It reflected off the falling water and created what looked like tiny sparkling flowers on everything that grew there. That one small ray against the waterfall illuminated the entire room. It had to be one of the most beautiful and breathtaking sights Sam or Matt had ever seen.

They walked closer to the edge of the pond to put out the torch. Before they reached the water, they felt a small short blast of wind from somewhere that extinguished the torch's flame. They both started looking around the edge of the pond. There was no dirt of any kind, no debris, or anything to diminish its beauty. Many different types of smaller fish could be seen swimming through the clear, crystal water or below near the sandy bottom.

Matt scooped up a handful of the clear soft water and put it to his lips. He smelled it to see if it was safe to drink. With a slow swift swiping motion of his tongue, he tasted it. He looked at Sam with a slight grin on his face, "I have never tasted water this good." He reached down to get more. Sam joined him "You're right. This is great."

They looked at each other and knew what they wanted to do. They removed their shirts and shoes and took a running jump over the bushes and into the cool clear water. It was very refreshing. They must have swum for at least an hour and a half. The water was so relaxing that they almost forgot they were on a search for Moses. They came out re-energized and decided to go for one last dive before leaving. They dove to the bottom of the pond that was approximately seventeen feet deep. They did some underwater searching. When they were about four feet from the bottom, they spotted an underwater cave entrance.

They returned to the surface. They each took a very large breath of air and headed back down and into the cave. The cave was about six feet in diameter and the walls were extremely smooth. Not too far into the cave, they noticed light above them. They went up to find an opening to another very large room. This room was also lit by a tiny ray of sunlight from a small hole high above in the ceiling. As they pulled themselves up to the surface, they could see the room was a giant berry patch. It seemed there were at least twelve to sixteen different sections, each containing its own type of berry. Matt, the outdoorsman, was the first to take a few from a couple of different bushes. He bit into them slowly and carefully to taste them. He nodded to Sam and, with a smile, said, "These berries are as tasty and refreshing as the water." Sam joined him and the two of them had an unexpected feast.

Shortly after eating the berries, they both passed out and everything was black. Each, in his own mind, wondered if he were dead or had just fallen asleep. Many hours had passed when Sam felt as if he were alive and awake. Sam could feel his eyes open, yet he could not see a thing. He yelled out for Matt but there was no answer. He tried feeling his way around, but all he could feel was the hard rock ground and the berry bushes. As Sam was feeling his way, he finally touched what he thought was another human being. Hopefully, it was Matt. He gently lifted the head and kept calling Matt's name in hopes that he would answer him. Sam kept slapping the cheeks and shaking the head. It seemed like forever until he finally received a reply in a familiar voice.

"What are you trying to do, kill me or something?"

They both laughed out loud. Then Matt asked Sam, "Who put out the lights?"

"Maybe it's nighttime and the sun has gone down."

They both chuckled again and told each other they were just glad to be alive and well. They fell asleep and woke again when the ray of the morning sun once again lit up the cave. As hungry as they were, they decided against eating those berries any time soon. They looked around, but could not find another opening except the one in the floor that they had discovered. The room was very quiet. Just as they were about to leave through the underwater cave, they thought they could hear voices. A greater light source started to fill the room. Everything was coming from a much bigger opening in the far wall than the one they had found. This one was even closer to the bottom. The voices were coming nearer. Sam and Matt stayed lying still on the floor. They could tell that the voices were those of very young children, but they could not hear what they were saying. Sam rose to his knees just in time to see two small people walking in the bright sunlight toward the opening. He and Matt jumped quickly to their feet and followed quietly at a safe distance. They waited until the two small people were out of sight and then they made a charge for the opening. Just as they were about to reach it, it closed. They looked and looked for hours, but could not find any way to make it open again. They waited to see if anyone would return. Nothing happened.

"Let's go back through the pond and return tomorrow. We can hide a little closer to the entrance to see if it opens again. If it does, we can try to sneak in without anyone noticing us." Matt said as he offered his plan to Sam.

"I was thinking we could do that." Sam said as he smiled in agreement.

They slipped into the water and swam to the large pond where they wrapped their shoes in their shirts and returned, once again, to the cave of the berry bushes. Night came and darkness fell. They hung their wet clothes and shoes over the bushes where they knew the morning sun would dry them.

The next morning, the entrance opened allowing the greater sunlight to enter. Sam and Matt saw two very pretty little girls, probably ten or eleven year's old carrying baskets. They began filling them with berries. They laughed and giggled as they merrily worked. Sam and Matt slipped through the opening and waited behind some trees, ready to follow the girls when they finished filling their baskets. As they waited for the girls, Matt and Sam were in awe of the beauty that surrounded them. It looked like a giant garden that was more beautiful than they had ever seen. There were flowers, bushes and trees of every kind. The air was filled with the harmonious singing of the birds. There were beautiful streams of water flowing gently over the rocks as if singing songs of their own. There were no signs of anything dead or dying; everything was in full bloom. There were stone paths that lead in many different directions without a weed between any of the stones. The stones were of many different shades, types and shapes. However, they were all flat enough for safe walking.

Sam could hear some voices coming from the path nearby. He tapped Matt to make sure he was aware that someone was coming. They stepped back into the bushes and knelt out of sight. Down the path came two men, two women and three little children. They were all talking and singing as they walked along the stones. Sam and Matt sat quietly a little longer. Soon, the same group came back and this time the two young girls from the berry cave were with them. Sam and Matt listened as the group passed by the bushes. The adults were telling the girls that they must hurry and return once they get the berries. They were told that mother and father would have to come get them if they kept the others waiting. The children apologized and were promising to be quicker the next time they went for berries.

Sam and Matt waited for a little while before stepping out and following them at a safe distance. They hadn't gone very far when they heard a larger group of people talking and yelling for the girls and their parents to hurry because everyone was waiting and ready to start.

Sam and Matt found a small group of bushes just atop a hill overlooking the crowd. They listened as the little group began eating and taking turns singing, telling stories or running off to play games. They truly looked like the happiest group of people that either Sam or Matt had ever come across. Their clothes appeared to be handmade and nothing like the store bought clothes Sam and Matt were used to. The area looked like a large courtyard with a huge wall around it similar to the one they had seen earlier on the other side of the caves. There were no buildings in sight. Sam looked at Matt, "Do you think this might possibly be some of the people we were reading about in the books we found back there? Matt replied, "Sam, let's get real, those people were of long ago." "Then what, do you think this could be a group on a nature hike or retreat of some kind"?"

Matt just shrugged his shoulders, "Don't know."

Sam noticed the sadness in Matt's face and wondered if he was thinking of his lost family. Then he saw Matt attempt a smile.

"Why don't we go down and introduce ourselves, Sam? At least they may be able to show us an easier way out of here. It is for sure they didn't all swim under that underwater cave."

"As you always say, 'Sounds like a plan to me'. Let's hope we don't frighten them."

Matt laughed and took one of his large hands and smoothed his hair and beard. Sam mocked him and did the same thing. Then they started down the hill.

One of the folks in the crowd saw them coming and yelled to the others. Everything stopped and all eyes were on Sam and Matt. Sam and Matt walked up to the first man they saw. They reached out their hands and made their introductions.

Sam started by asking all the questions, "Where is your group from? What are all of you doing out here so far from everything?"

Then Matt joined in and explained some of the dangers the group might encounter. The man listened to both of them and then said, "It is very nice to meet both of you. I am John Winslow. To answer your question, we are from here. Here is where we live. What do you mean, being this far away from everything?"

"Here?" Sam looked puzzled. "Where are all your houses?"

Mr. Winslow just pointed toward the base of the far wall and said in a very strong voice, "There."

One of the little girls walked over and gently took hold of Sam's hand and led him farther down the path toward the outer wall. As they neared the wall, Sam could see what looked like windows and doors carved into the hill side. He was a little confused because he could see no sunrise on the other side. The little girl brought him closer and opened a door that led into a very large and beautiful room surrounded by many different kinds of flowers and evergreen greenery. One of the parents brought Matt into the room.

As Sam and Matt were being welcomed, they were asked "Where do you live? We thought no one else existed."

"What!" Sam laughed. "No one else existed? Is that what you just said?"

"Yes of course!" was the reply. "We would also like to know how you got here."

Matt asked, "Who is your leader? Maybe I need to talk to him or her first?"

"Leader? What do you mean?"

Sam, who couldn't believe what he was hearing, tried to explain. "A leader. Someone who is in charge of everything. Someone who makes and enforces all the rules. Anyone like that here?"

"No. We have no such thing as a leader. We are all equal."

Sam just looked at Matt in disbelief.

Everyone sat around a very large campfire while Matt explained where they lived. He told them that there were millions of people just like them all over the world. He told them that they were looking for Moses, Sam's dog.

Sam could see by the expressions of their faces that they found it difficult to believe what Matt was telling them.

Sam decided to ask them again. "Where are you from?" He received the same answer, "Here, here. We've always been from here?"

Sam pulled Matt aside and told him how much this resembled the other area they were in, and that these people may be the remainder of that civilization. Matt pushed his glasses back high on his nose and gave Sam a very strange look. "I think you've been reading too many of your own articles, my friend." They returned quickly to the group.

Then, one of the parents started to explain. "Years ago, the large hole in the cave came and took many of our peoples' lives. The big hole inside just swallowed them. They were pulled over the edge while they were picking berries. They were never seen again."

A little boy standing nearby with tears in his eyes said, "One of them was my grandfather. I never got to know him." They went on to say that the area of the city was much smaller now then it had been generations ago. There were only a few books that had survived some kind of a major flood of some kind.

Matt then interrupted and said that they had found some books and would bring them the next time they came. The joy that Matt's statement made on their faces could have lit up one of the caves they had come through earlier.

Sam and Matt listened while everyone tried to assure them that this was all they had ever known. They insisted that they never knew that anything or anyone else existed.

Sam was astonished. He said "If one of you can open the entrance to the cave for us, we can go and return with pictures that will show you we are telling the truth."

"There is no known way of opening the cave. It just opens at a certain time of day when the sun's reflection is at a particular position in the sky. Then it closes as the sun disappears behind the high wall that surrounds the city. It happens at the same time each day unless something prevents the sun's rays from reflecting on the opening. That has only happened twice as far as I can remember".

Someone else in the group added, "It was only adults who were swallowed by the big hole. That is why adults do not enter the cave, anymore. We send the children to pick the berries. They seem to be safe."

Another person spoke, "The berries are good for cooking and eating. We also use them as medicine. They help keep us from getting sick. We have to be careful, though, because eating too many berries will put you in a deep sleep. We are not sure, but we think too many of them might kill you."

Sam smiled at Matt. He wondered if either of them would ever eat a berry again.

"You should consider going out the way you came. You don't want to risk being swallowed up by the big hole and never be seen again."

Matt tried to assure them "That is how we got here, through the big hole."

Again, the people asked them how they got there through the cave. They said they had no knowledge of any other openings. Matt and Sam continued to try to convince them that they had come from the same hole everyone claimed had swallowed their people.

It was getting late and Matt and Sam explained they wanted to get an early start in the morning. They said they would return as soon as they could. Before going to sleep, Matt and Sam discussed whether or not they would share any of this with people outside of here. They also tried to think of what they would bring back when they returned. They were anxious to prove to the people of the village that both of them could leave and return safely.

When daylight came, Sam and Matt were busily preparing for their journey. Many of the people pleaded with them not to go. They offered to have them stay and make their home there. Matt and Sam tried to assure them that they would be fine and return as soon as they could. Everything was ready. The sun was peeking over the wall. Soon, the entrance was open and Matt and Sam were waving farewell. The people of the village did not want them to leave. They were afraid that this was the last time they would ever see either of them again. They all returned to their homes. The next day when the girls entered the cave, there were no signs of Sam or Matt. When the little girls reported back to the village people, everyone was very sad.

Sam and Matt found their way back to the long narrow path that led them to the campsite. Sam quickly packed up his camera and many of the pictures he had developed, including some of Moses and Quickshaw. Sam lingered over Moses' picture and whispered, "I miss you, boy."

Sam watched as Matt packed a few things including a flashlight, radio and some binoculars. When Matt was finished he said "Let's go. This should be interesting."

They rushed back in the direction of the cave. Sam's mind was racing almost as fast as his feet. "Do you think these pictures will finally convince them that there is life outside of their world? Do you think they can handle that?"

Matt replied, "Don't know. One thing I know for sure. They'll see that it's possible to go in and out of that big hole without being 'swallowed up'."

Sam wanted to help the people to understand what was going on in the world, but he was also anxious to resume the search for Moses.

Sam and Matt timed it so they would be in the water cave and up in the berry patch during the sunlight hours. About three days had passed before they were able to get back to the area. They had packed the camera and pictures in waterproof packaging and made their way to the pond at the foot of the waterfall. They placed their clothes in the same type of waterproof container and swam to the underwater cave that brought them to the berry patch. They quickly made their way to the area near the cave opening. As soon as the sun opened it, they were back on the stone path that led to the village.

Sam tried to keep pace with Matt and his long legged strides as they made their way up the path across the bubbling brooks and all the beautiful greenery. Sam could not wait to see how the people would react when they saw that Matt and he had safely returned.

As they came to the top of the hill, they heard a little child from the village yelling, "They're back! They're back! Everyone come see. They're back!"

What a thrill it was for Sam and Matt to hear that little excited voice calling to the rest of the village. Then they heard screams of joy as they came down from the hill. A few of the villagers ran off in another direction as if in fear of seeing a ghost or something of a Godly nature that they did not understand. The rest of the people greeted them with tears, smiles and open arms. They were genuinely glad to see them again. It was quite a reunion. They had an entire day of celebration. It was a day that seemed like it would never end. Sam confided in Matt, "I have never before felt so missed or so loved." Matt nodded, but could say nothing. Sam noticed a small tear running down Matt's cheek.

Finally, they made their way to the center of the village and were invited to stay with the same couple as last time. Sam and Matt could not have been treated any better. Their hosts, Tad and Lindsay, were very friendly and extremely kind. A delicious lunch was prepared and all were asked to come outside to a large picnic table and enjoy it. During lunch, Sam learned that the two little girls were named Melinda and Megan and the little boy was called Ethan. After thoroughly enjoying lunch, Sam shared his pictures with the entire family. The adults looked at them first and then they passed them around the table to their children. The three children smiled as they stared at the Moses and Quickshaw. Melinda said "We've seen the eagle many times, but we never realized he had a name or that he belonged to someone."

Amazingly, while they were talking about Quickshaw, they saw him flying high above the top of the great wall. He flew down and landed on a small branch just behind Matt's chair.

A child nearby became a little frightened. Matt tried to assure him, "Please, don't be afraid. Quickshaw won't hurt you. Come here. Would you like to pat him?" The child, with very small tears in his eyes, refused Matt's offer.

Then, Quickshaw jumped onto Matt's forearm and just stared at him. Matt hung his head and said "We've spent a lot of time looking for him, Quickshaw, but we haven't found him yet."

Matt handed the children some bread and crackers and asked if they would like to feed Quickshaw. Most of them did not want to try. Too them, Quickshaw was a very big, scary eagle. Ethan had a different perspective. He saw Quickshaw as a friendly, domesticated bird. He stepped closer to Matt. He began stroking Quickshaw's back with a soft, slow, swiping motion. Quickshaw didn't seem to mind. He stayed in one position and appeared to be enjoying the attention. Then he slowly and gently shook his wings to let Ethan know it was time to stop. Ethan stepped backwards. Quickshaw quickly flew to the top of the great wall and then continued his search for Moses.

Sam continued passing out pictures for everyone to see. The more they looked at them, the more they were in disbelief. They had never seen the many wonders Sam had captured with this strange instrument he referred to as a camera. The children were told they could each pick one to keep. It was difficult for the children to choose just one, but they did. They agreed they would all share with each other. Hearing their little excited voices really pleased Sam.

The rest of the day, Sam, Matt and the adults discussed the huge differences between the two worlds. Sam said "I know it seems difficult to conceive. After all, we are just miles apart and only separated by a single entrance through a pond. This pond leads to the underwater cave and then through your berry patch. The berry patch then leads to the cave door that opens at the command of the sun." Sam was hoping they understood exactly how he and Matt were able to find them.

The campfires burned late that night and the stories continued to flow until the early morning hours. Stories, on both sides, were filled with excitement and adventure. Each side of the great wall had its good and bad points. There were differences of opinions as to which world was truly civilized. It wasn't clear, at this point, who would want the other's world.

They all agreed with Sam and Matt that the village was better left a secret for the time being. It was not for them to decide that night, what to do or where to go from there. For now, they agreed to be the best of friends and visit as time allowed. They wanted everything to remain as it was. They wanted to try to have the people in the village stay within its walls until more discussions and decisions could be made. No one wanted to see the simple way of life in the village, with all its natural beauty, compromised and commercialized. Sam knew this beautiful area could even be destroyed forever if the wrong people were to get knowledge of its existence.

Sam and Matt stayed a few more days and then left to continue their search for Moses. As difficult as it was, Sam did not keep any of the pictures he took of the villagers and their breathtaking surroundings; he left them for the people to keep. The children seemed to enjoy the pictures the most. They loved seeing what they looked like through the eyes of a camera. They stared in disbelief, laughing and giggling as they showed each other the funny poses Sam had captured while they were working or playing. Before he left, he assured the villagers that he and Matt were not taking any pictures with them. He reassured them that he would keep this area a secret. He and Matt promised they would return one day soon.

Before long, Sam and Matt were back in the part of the cave where the giant waterfall and pond were located. They had not moved very far down the cave when they saw a large vine hanging from the high ceiling.

"Did you see this before, Matt?

"Nope, missed that one."

Sam and Matt looked around to see what else they may have missed. Just below the hanging vine was a very narrow gulley that looked like it had no bottom. There was a narrow ledge on the side across from them. As they were looking at each other, Sam asked, "Do you see that large rock?"

Since Matt could see several large rocks there, he simply asked "Which one?"

Sam pointed and said, "The second from the right. See! Look at the ground near it. It looks like it has been moved at one time or another. I'll bet it is some kind of door."

Sam and Matt looked more closely at the area. They could see the familiar looking ivy with its beautiful colors, again. It was partially covering the wall. It extended down to the edge of the waterfall. While Sam was still assessing the situation, Matt used the vine to try to get to the other side. As soon as his weight was on the vine, he started to swing across the narrow gulley. Simultaneously, the rock on the other side began to move very slowly. When Matt reached the other side, he noticed that the rock had completely moved. Sam gasped and said, "I knew it!"

There was very large opening right in front of both of them. Before Matt could let go of the rope, he saw Moses leap out with the greatest excitement ever. Sam fell to his knees and cried with joy. He never thought he would ever see Moses again. Matt released the vine and ran to Moses to give him a hug. The door began to close. Sam yelled "Matt, watch out!" The large rock was slowly heading toward Matt and Moses. If it hit them, they would be dragged very close to the edge of the narrow gulley. Sam was afraid that it might even push them over the edge.

When Matt heard Sam yell, he instinctively grabbed the vine again. As he did, the rock came to a stand still. Moses went back behind the large rock, where he had been trapped, and took a running start. He was able to leap across the narrow gulley to safety. Once again, he was at Sam's side. Matt, too, took a running start. In just a few seconds, he was on the other side with Sam and Moses. The three of them embraced. Sam and Matt couldn't stop telling Moses how much they had missed him and how they really thought that they would never see him again. Neither Sam nor Matt had verbalized that until now.

As he was continuing to pat Moses, Sam thought about what Moses had just experienced. He must have been playing with the vine until he found himself on the other side. Then he probably sniffed his way into the cave right before the door closed behind him. Sam couldn't imagine how Moses felt while he was all alone trapped behind that door. "Looks like you found water in there, boy. Good dog, good dog!"

Matt reached in his pocket and pulled out a handful of dog biscuits he had been carrying. Sam laughed and pulled out a whole fist full of dog goodies. Moses was in his glory and was content to just sit a while and enjoy being spoiled. Both Sam and Matt smiled at Moses and patted him on the head. They were each telling him it great to have him back. They also made it clear that he was never to wander off like that again.

Sam took a moment and said, "Thanks, Matt. Thanks for being such a good friend and sticking with me all the time I was searching for Moses."

Matt looked at Sam and then down at Moses and said with a smile, "He isn't just your dog anymore. He's our dog."

Sam embraced Matt and with tear filled eyes. "You're right, my friend. You're right!"

The three of them went down the cave with the intent of coming back later to search the area where Moses had been confined. Then they could learn what he had experienced while he was trapped.

Soon they were outside in the sunny, fresh, clear air. They were on the path to the campsite. Matt stopped for a moment and gave out a very loud scream. Quickshaw came over the hill and down through the trees until he was at Matt's side. Quickshaw soon made his way to Moses' feet. He pecked at his left jaw as if giving him a kiss. There was no doubt that Quickshaw was just as happy to see Moses again. Then he quickly flew to a high limb on a nearby tree. When he flew back, he laid two small dog biscuits at Moses' feet just in front of him, in case he was hungry. Sam and Matt laughed aloud and patted both of them.

As they headed down the path, Quickshaw was poking and picking at Moses as they slowly and excitedly walked back to the familiar areas once again. They could stop at the campsite just long enough to pack and get started back to Matt's place before the sun set. It didn't take them long to get all their belongings together before they were on their way. Quickshaw went on ahead and disappeared into the beautiful blue sky high over the hills.

On the way to Matt's cabin, they went through town to pick up some badly needed supplies. They also wanted to catch up on any news. While they were in the general store, Sam noticed that Matt was being teased by some of the townsfolk. They were taunting him about some of the hikes he takes and the fact that he lives all alone in the hills. Some jested and called him their modern-day Davy Crockett. Others even laughed and called him Daniel Boone. Still others, because of his big size, called him their very own Paul Bunyan. Some even made cracks, "You know ole Matt probably found that village of weirdo's that old Hank Scott rants and raves about every time he has nothing else to say. Often times, when Hank wanted to be part of our conversations, he would tell us this crazy story about where he came from many years ago."

Another would comment that he and Matt were probably two of the nuttiest people they had ever met. Everyone agreed it was good that both of them lived outside of town. They said that Hank had probably married some ugly woman from that hidden city and was trying to keep her hidden, too. They even suggested that maybe Matt and Hank were somehow related, but just had nothing to do with each other.

Matt and Sam had no comments about any of it and just stayed out of the conversations altogether. They bought the supplies they wanted, paid what they owed and headed out of the store. Paul Jenkins told them not to pay any attention to the jesting. He said no one meant anything by it.

Once outside and on the road to Matt's place, they began to discuss Hank Scott. They wondered what he might know, if anything, or if he had just made up a story that sounded like the place they had visited. They decided that Hank's place might be a good trip for the next day. They spent the night relaxing with a nice long warm bath and a hot cup of fresh coffee. They shared events of the local newspaper. They all had a good long sleep, including Moses. They arose with the morning sun. Sam was the first one awake. By the time Matt awoke, Sam had coffee and breakfast ready. They had breakfast, packed a couple of supplies and headed out to find where this Hank Scott fellow lived. Mr. Jenkins, from the store, gave them directions to get to Hank's place. When they arrived, they found no building. There was a corral, some chickens, beautiful plants, a small stream and a stone path that led to the side of a very large mountain. They followed the path and yelled out for Hank as they walked. As they came closer to the mountain, they could see a cave house similar to the one in the secret village they had just visited. A man came out and asked what he could do for them and what they wanted. They told him they were just passing through and were hoping to get a nice tall glass of clear cold spring water.

Hank was very friendly and invited them into the house cave where he lived. Sam and Matt were looking around in a very curious manner and it made Hank a little uneasy. He broke the silence by asking, "What about the dog? Was he thirsty, too? Should I give him a bowl of water?" Sam replied, "Sure thanks."

Sam and Matt stayed long enough to see that there were a lot of similarities between Hank and the village they had visited. They were hesitant to ask him any questions. They thought they should just leave Hank alone and avoid prying into his private life. It was difficult to leave Hank without knowing if he had any ties to the village people or if he had even seen the village. They thanked Hank for everything and, as hard as it was to leave without asking questions, they were on their way. Moses followed closely behind.

A few weeks had passed and Matt and Sam were ready to go on a hike that should give them enough information and photographs to finish up Sam's article. Almost everything was packed and they were just closing everything when there was a knock at the door. It was Hank Scott. He said he had just dropped by to ask them a couple of questions. Someone in town had given him directions. He said, "I left early this morning in hopes of spending some time with both of you."

Hank, noticing that they were already packed, said he could return another time if they preferred. Sam and Matt looked at each other. Moses went back to lying in front of the now cooled fireplace. Matt started a small fire outside and put on a pot of coffee. They put all the gear aside and pulled up a couple of old wooden chairs from the shed. Sam got the cups and the coffee was ready in a jiffy. They all sat back and Matt told Hank he was glad that he stopped by to visit and asked what they could do for him. They talked about the weather, the scenery, hiking, cooking, animals and everything except what they really had on their minds. No one wanted to be the first to bring up the subject of the village and the inhabitants. Night came and Hank spent the night on Matt's front porch.

# Chapter 3

# The Return of Hank Scott

It was bright and early on a Monday morning and Hank was waiting as Sam and Matt came out for breakfast. The chairs were still in place next to the campfire. Everyone grabbed a chair, pulled it up to the table and had a hardy meal. Hank began telling Matt and Sam that he, too, had always wanted to go hiking, but knew of no one else who could go with him. Then he asked if he could tag along on one of the hikes with them. Sam and Matt both assured Hank that he would be welcomed anytime he would like to join them. They said they were on their way out today and had to get going. Maybe the next time they would give him some notice so he would be ready to join them.

Hank couldn't thank them enough and said, "You mean if I had been ready this time, I could have joined you?"

Sam looked at Matt for his approval and said, "Of course."

Hank sprung to his feet, went running across the yard, dashed behind a tree and came back with a knapsack and a bag filled with things for camping. He returned quickly to the breakfast table. They all laughed wholeheartedly. Moses was barking as if joining in the laughter. Quickshaw showed up to see why there was so much excitement. He rested on the back of Matt's chair. Matt introduced Quickshaw to Hank.

Breakfast was over and the three of them were ready to start their new hiking adventure joined by the two loyal pets. They hiked about ten miles and decided to make camp for the day. The air was fresh and beautiful and a gentle breeze was coming in from the east. Moses snuggled close to the rock that Sam had decided to use as a chair. It was very quiet and peaceful as they sat back to decide on the plan and direction for the next day. While Matt and Sam were discussing what they hoped to find, Hank jumped in and asked to hear of some of the places they had been and some of the things that they had seen. Hank also asked if he might look through some of the photos Sam had taken on previous trips.

While Hank skimmed through the pictures one by one, Matt and Sam made a campfire and started cooking dinner. Hank couldn't take his eyes off the pictures. By the time he decided to eat, his supper was cold and Matt and Sam were nearly ready for bed. Hank then commented to Sam that he didn't seem to have any pictures of people in his collection and he asked why. Sam gulped and took time to explain to Hank that his article really was intended to be on animals, nature and just naturally created beauty. Hank continued his questioning, "Don't you consider a person to be a naturally created beauty?"

Sam again gulped and slowly answered, "Yes. Yes, of course I do. People are probably the greatest example of all, but my assignment for the magazine article was to be on nature."

The two men looked at each other for a moment and then looked away as Matt broke the silence by letting them know there was a herd of Moose passing by on the other side of the ravine. Hank and Sam leaped to their feet and came to the edge of the clearing. They could see about two hundred moose running in a great hurry as if they had a destination in mind. Once the herd was out of sight, everyone went back to the campfire to turn in for the evening. The night was clear and the sky was filled with millions of bright, sparkling stars. The next morning, however, brought with it a heavy fog and dampness in the air. They quickly packed and started on their way. As the day passed, the weather became worse. The rain began to pour with thunder and lightening booming all around them. They looked for shelter and found a dry cave on the side of a hill. They immediately got out of the rain and started a small campfire to try to dry themselves. It was quite a downpour and it looked as if it would never stop. They decided to settle in and make the best of it.

Later, they all fell asleep. Sam was the first to wake. He found the campfire had gone out and the cave was completely dark. He grabbed a match from his pocket, some paper, a few twigs and restarted the fire. Suddenly, he noticed that where the cave entrance once was, there was now no more opening. Sam crawled over and woke Matt and Hank. He shared his discovery with them. The three looked at each other and couldn't understand how such a mud slide could have occurred without awakening at least one of them. The opening was covered with mud, rocks and very large tree branches. As they tried to remove some of it to clear the entrance, more would just fall in its place. Even after hours of work, they had not made a dent. It seemed that all they had managed to do was fill up the cave with what they had removed from the entrance.

Sam and Hank decided to continue trying to clear it while Matt checked out the rest of the cave to see if there was another way out. Moses accompanied Matt to provide him some protection. The only thing Matt could find was a very long narrow tunnel that looked like it went clear up to heaven. The space was so small only Moses could fit in it; perhaps he could go for help. Matt instructed Moses and helped him get started up the long narrow opening. Once he saw Moses make it to the top, he hurried back to tell Sam and Hank of his plan.

The three of them kept working and trying to clear the opening. Sam and Hank would pull it away from the opening and Matt would drag it farther into the cave out of the way. They worked for hours and finally came to a spot that was beginning to feel dry. They all needed a break and sat back to rest for a few moments. They weren't sure if Moses would be able to get anyone to follow him, especially if they knew he was with Matt. No one really wanted anything to do with them. They had to keep trying. There was no other way. They continued for many more hours and still no sign of sunlight. All of them were so exhausted, they fell asleep. They awoke at different times. Matt was the first to awake and put more wood on the fire. Sam was second and put on the coffee. When Hank awoke, he shared the coffee and biscuits with them. They talked about a new plan to keep working in shifts to avoid a complete stand still.

Again, as they worked, hours passed and it seemed there was no end in sight. Hank had about all he could take. Sam certainly wasn't used to this kind of physical work. He, too, was exhausted and ready to quit. Matt told them to take a break, catch their breath and he would continue on for a while. Hank headed down the cave again to double check and see if perhaps Matt had missed a turn or something the first time he looked. When Hank returned, he told Sam and Matt the original cave entrance was also the only exit. He said that if they couldn't clear it, this could be their home for a long time to come.

Matt finally needed a break. Hank agreed to work for a while and made his way back to the pile of debris. After he was digging for quite some time, he stopped and yelled to Matt and Sam, "I think I can hear something or someone digging on the other side."

"Maybe Moses persuaded the townspeople to follow him." Sam said. He may have crossed some other campers' path and was able to get them to come."

The three of them had a new energy and began to give it their all. Suddenly, a ray of sunlight came through where Hank was digging. Then he saw the claw of a bear. He quickly jumped back and told Sam and Matt that this cave must belong to a bear and maybe their troubles were just beginning.

Matt came to the area where Hank was digging and sure enough, as he bent to dig, he saw the claw of what looked like a very large bear come through with each swipe. They decided that the bear was going to be in there and that they had better hide behind all the debris. They decided to let the bear come in and then run quickly out as he went by them. It sounded like a good plan. No sooner were they well hidden when the big black bear come crashing through followed by a slightly smaller bear and two little cubs. When they saw the clear opening, they made a dash through it and thought they were free. The big bear's claw grabbed Matt on his way by and locked him in his arms. The big black bear, with Matt locked in his arms, rolled out of the cave and onto the ground. Matt looked up with the fear of God on his face just in time to see Moses there licking his cheeks. The bear let go of Matt and gave him a swift hit on the shoulder and sent him rolling across the ground to a big old oak tree. The big black bear then stood up on his hind legs and looked like he was going to attack when Matt noticed how familiar the bear looked. This was the same big black bear from a long time ago and this must be his family. Moses had found him and brought him to help again. They all had a good laugh as the bears went on their way. Matt and Sam shared the story with Hank who was still in shock, but relieved at the same time. He was just happy to be free. Hank said he had, had an experience similar to this years ago, when he thought he was going to die. However, that time, he would have been drowned in an underwater cave. Matt and Sam asked Hank to tell them about it, but he just wasn't ready. Everyone gave Moses a hug and thanked him for his courage. They congratulated him for finding the big black bear and his family. If not for them, they may never have been seen again.

The sun was bright and the day was clear, but it was coming to a close pretty fast. They retrieved their goods from the cave, set up their tents and had supper. They thanked God that they all were still alive. Then they settled in for a good night's sleep.

Because they were so tired, they slept until noon the next day. Nothing could have or would have been able to wake them once their eyes were closed. When they did awake, they each had a new energy sparked by the beautiful weather. They went to see where their journey would bring them. As they walked along the edge of a stream filled with fish leaping for bugs above its surface, they felt nothing could be more beautiful. They could see frogs and turtles along the river bank and birds flying and singing as they soared smoothly in the sky.

Many beautiful sights were seen during the day as they continued to walk. The lakes, rivers, streams and springs flowing down the side of a hill gave them all a comforting feeling. They could see the mountains in the distance that seemed to beckon them to come and see the beauty they, too, held. Nature was showing off its beauty all around them and begging them to take a closer look. Sam thought he had taken enough equipment for this ten day trip, however, he was already running out of film. They had only been gone a couple of days. That afternoon the three of them sat and talked about what they might like to do if they had extra time. Matt said he would like to just sit in a small boat or canoe in the middle of the lake and listen to the waves banging up against its sides. He loved being in a boat in the middle of the lake, especially at sunset. He said there was nothing more beautiful then the sun going down behind the mountains with the bright orange, yellow and purples that usually came with the setting of the sun. Sam said he would like to climb the highest tree with Moses on his back and see as far as he could and just take in all of nature's beauty. Moses barked in agreement. Hank, with tears in his eyes, expressed a desire to find relatives he had not seen in years. Matt asked him about his relatives. Hank was a little hesitant to confide in them because it seemed no one had ever believed him. Sam encouraged him to tell his story. He promised Hank that he and Matt would not laugh or judge him one way or the other. It took Hank a long time to think and then he finally cleared his throat and began to speak.

"It was many years ago and in what now seems like a perfect land. It was a simple life and a place where everyone loved everyone and they all had pretty much the same thing. Whatever there was, it was to be shared by all. There were no rich, no poor, no leaders, no followers and no one ever laughed at one another."

Hank talked on for hours about this place he remembered, but said it all seemed like a dream now. He even questioned if such a place ever existed. Sam and Matt wanted to tell him about their recent experience, but decided to ask a few more questions first.

Sam spoke up, "Hank, tell us. How did you ever come to leave this place and why did you never go back?"

Hank went on to explain that he remembers that a number of them were together when there was a great opening in the huge wall that surrounded their city. Some of them went through the opening and found beautiful and tasty berries. However, while they were in there, the great wall closed and it was very dark. He said he had stumbled into a bed of water and hit his head. After that he has no idea what happened until he was awakened at the campfire of some hikers from town. They nursed him back to health and took him back to town. When he recovered, he rambled on about where he was from and how he wanted to get back to his people where he belonged. He said the more he talked, the more people thought he was crazy. Finally, they just began to ignore him and left him alone outside of town.

"What happened to the others that were with you?" asked Matt.

Hank stopped for a minute, looked at both Sam and Matt and told them maybe he better stop his story before they, too, would ignore him and leave him out in this unknown wilderness. Sam came close to Hank, smiled and softly told him, "We believe every word you said. Why haven't you ever tried to return?"

Hank told them he wouldn't know where to begin. He said he never saw where he came from or how to get there. The hikers treated him as a crazy person and refused to have anything to do with him. They were afraid to even talk to him for fear that they, too, would become insane.

Matt started to tell the story of how Moses got lost on a hiking trip and the many days they spent searching caves trying to find him. He told Hank how, during that time, they had come across a body of water with a great waterfall. He mentioned that beneath the waterfall was an underwater cave that led to a berry patch. Matt continued to tell of what happened to them when they ate too many berries. He told him of the great wall opening to the beautiful city that existed behind it. The beauty that existed there was far greater than any they had ever seen, because it was natural and real. Hank was crying out of control as he listened to Matt's fantastic story of the city behind the caves.

Still weeping, he said, "Oh thank God! Thank God!"

It took many hours to get Hank to settle down. They offered to help him find his way back to his wonderful homeland.

The next day they headed across a piece of land that was a new route for Matt. He knew it would be almost a direct route back to where they could get home and pick up some fresh supplies. He felt this route would save a lot of travel time. As they journeyed along, Sam kept feeling they were being watched. Even Moses was acting very jumpy. They each kept an eye out as they walked along this new path. Soon, they came to an opening that looked as though someone had been there recently. They made a campfire. Just as they were about to sit down, they heard something that sounded like screaming in the bushes behind them. Moses was tugging at something, but they couldn't see what.

The three of them arrived on the scene to see what was happening. When they pushed back the bushes, they found a man shaking and shivering with fear. They were gently trying to help him into the clearing, when four other men jumped out to his aid and asked that he be not harmed. Hank was looking strangely at one of them. As he continued to stare at the man, he said, "Herman, is that you? Can that really be you?"

The man, with tears in his eyes, softly returned the question, "Hank! Hank, can that really be you?"

Suddenly all four men were hugging and rejoicing. The afternoon was spent with introductions and explanations of where each had been and what each had been doing for the many passed years. Hank introduced them one at a time, Herman, Jake, Andrew, Michael and John. They explained how they, too, had been discovered wondering aimlessly. At first, they were helped by others until they were considered insane and sent on their way. They were fortunate enough to come across each other. They decided to stay together until they could figure out what to do. Somehow, they managed to get by all this time. Now, they were overwhelmed at the fact that finally, someone might be able to help them get back home to their loved ones. Each of these men was getting on in years and certainly not in tip-top shape. They also questioned Hank as to how well he knew Matt and Sam and if they could be trusted. They wanted to make certain they were not up to something. Hank assured them that they were all in good hands. He said that Matt and Sam would help them however they could.

They all traveled to a point that was half way between Matt's cottage and the hidden city. They made camp while Matt and Hank went back for supplies. Sam stayed behind to keep the group company until they returned. Then they would continue the journey. The men were getting very excited about going back home. They spent the evening sharing stories with Sam about their families. Each and every story was filled with nothing but love and admiration for one another. Sam believed them all because he had been there and had experienced it. Sam told them about one of the wonderful little boys he had met while in their city. He said his name was Ethan and his only sadness was that he never knew his grandfather. Andrew perked up and said that's kind of nice to know that someone there has used my father's name for their son. My wife never cared for the name so we named our only son Tad. The stories continued without stopping.

Matt and Hank returned with enough supplies to get the journey underway. Since everyone was pretty well rested, they started their trek at first sunrise. The day was beautiful and the temperature was just right. There was a gentle breeze that made it easy to walk without tiring too quickly. The journey was hard on everyone, but the excitement of getting home helped them to keep up a good pace. They moved right along. Finally, they came to an area that was getting close to the caves. They decided to make camp and schedule everything so that, hopefully, they would arrive in the cave's berry patch around the time the sun would be opening the large stone door. Matt decided that it would be a good idea to let the people in the hidden city know they were brining the men back. They weren't sure how it would affect everyone if they were to just show up. He called for Quickshaw and tied a note to his neck. Quickshaw flew high up and disappeared into the grayish darkness of the night.

When Quickshaw had came to the campsite that night for a visit he was introduced to everyone. They mentioned that Quickshaw had already been to the hidden city many times. Herman and the others were glad to make Quickshaw's acquaintance. Herman said that he wished they could just get up and fly over the walls to their families. The next morning they all made the journey inside the cave as far as the waterfall with the pond. They made camp there and the planned to go the rest of the way early the next morning. Matt had brought ropes with him. His plan was that he was going to swim through the underwater cave to the other side and secure the ropes so they could pull themselves through quickly.

The men from the hidden city were a little concerned. The last time they were in water, they were separated from their families for years. They didn't want that to ever happen again. Matt swam to the other side, secured the rope and swam back to show them they had nothing to fear. He said that it wouldn't take very long once they were in the water. All was set. They slept very little that night because of all the excitement about finally going home. Morning came and all were ready to proceed. Hank offered to go first and help give the others a sense of security that all was going to go well. Before long, Hank was in the water and in the berry grove. For the first time in many years he was in familiar surroundings and very close to home. Soon everyone was in the berry grove, in dry clothing, excitingly awaiting the opening of the big cave door. The time came. The first ray of sunshine shone through as it began to move. They all made their way closer to the door. When it opened, without hesitation, they were all back in their homeland.

There was not a soul in sight. It was agreed that Sam would go first to forewarn everyone they had arrived. He ran as fast as he could. As they approached the city, Hank and the others could hear loud cries of excitement coming from over the hill. The feelings were overwhelming. Sam and Matt just tried to stay in the background and enjoy the moment. There were enough happy tears to create another lake. Once things were almost back to normal, a great feast was planned. Tad and Lindsey were introducing Ethan and the girls to Herman, their grandfather. What a glorious day and evening it was! They prayed that any others out there would also survive and be brought home one day.

Hank came to Sam and Matt that night and explained that he didn't know how to repay, or thank them for all they had done. Matt and Sam had assured Hank they had been well paid for whatever they did many times over, just by the joy they had seen, experienced here today. They felt it was such a privilege just to know of this village and the wonderful people. They did have one request. Now that Hank knew of some of the ways of the outside world, would he please never allow it to change anything here. Hank assured them that he and the others had seen enough and would never let that happen to their city. Quickshaw once again, showed up for the celebration. This time all of the children took turns feeding him. They laughed and told him if he kept eating like that, he would never be able to get high enough to clear the big wall when he wanted to leave. The children were also petting, feeding and playing with Moses. They kept telling him how much they loved him.

Sam, Moses, Matt and Quickshaw stayed for another couple of days and then were ready to make their way back to their side of the great caves. Everyone in the city told them they were sad to see them leave, but would look forward to their return one day soon. Again, it was agreed that the hidden city would remain hidden. The following day, they left with hugs and kisses from everyone. That night, Sam and Matt camped in the same spot and wondered if they were making a mistake by going back home. Over the next few months, Sam and Matt came across grave sites that they felt may be some of the people from the hidden city. They would write the names down and have Quickshaw deliver the news over the great wall.

# Chapter 4

## The Fire

Sam and Matt took their time getting home so they could get the rest of the pictures needed to finish Sam's magazine article. Within a day, they had all that Sam felt he needed. They soon were back in familiar surroundings and were back at Matt's cabin. They were finally ready to settle in for a while and just take it easy. Sam spent most of the afternoon getting everything ready for his trip to the city. He had completed his project for the magazine. That night, Sam and Matt discussed all the fun and excitement they had while trying to get the pictures together. They both agreed the best story was the story that could never be told along with the best pictures that could never be published.

While they were reminiscing, they heard a knock at the door. It was the local sheriff. He was with a couple of the townspeople and was asking about Hank Scott. The sheriff explained that the townspeople were concerned because the last time they saw Hank, he was asking about directions to Matt's place. Matt said, "Hank did drop by a while back just to say 'hello'. He told me that he was heading back home and probably wouldn't be seeing me again."

The sheriff asked Matt why Hank would stop by to tell him, but no one else. "Where did he say his home was?"

Matt indicated that Hank didn't name the town. One of the townspeople spoke up and said, "You two probably killed him and buried him somewhere."

Another said, "Where did you take him? To the hidden city?"

And still another, "Why would he come and tell you? You didn't even know each other!"

They continued with one accusing question after another until the sheriff told everyone to just calm down. They looked around Matt's place until they were convinced that Hank was not there. They also checked the grounds, but found nothing that looked like a newly dug grave. The sheriff looked at Matt and told him he would be keeping an eye on him so he'd better start watching his step. The townspeople were not happy with the sheriff at all and they let him know it. They also indicated that if he couldn't or wouldn't take action against Matt then maybe they would have to take matters in their own hands. The sheriff sent them all on their way. When they were clearly out of sight, he left.

Before leaving for the train the next morning, Sam tried to talk Matt into going away with him for a while until things calmed down. Matt thanked him for the offer and the concern, but refused to be chased away from his home. A flood did that to him one day and took everything he loved. He wasn't about to let people do the same. Quickshaw had sensed that Sam and Moses were leaving and swooped in to say good-bye. It was a very sad time for all. They had been through a lot together. Sam stopped as he made his way down the front steps and offered to leave Moses for a while. He said it would give him a good reason to return. Again, Matt thanked him, but told him to get on his way before he missed his train. Sam left down the road and soon he and Moses were out of sight and on the train going home. Quickshaw followed the train for a couple of miles and then turned back to his friend who was sitting alone on his front porch.

It was a very long and lonely ride back to the city for Sam, but he had a great story and some great memories that would last a life time. The train made one stop and a man was brought on the train in handcuffs. He and two deputies sat in the seat just behind Sam. Moses was sitting on the seat just across from Sam and had been very still before now. The man smiled softly at Moses and Moses perked up as if he knew him. Sam patted him on the head and told him to be still. Moses lay back on his seat. Sam could hear the deputies questioning the man in handcuffs about where he was from and why he just happened to be at the back of the bank while it was being robbed. The man was explaining to the deputies that he was just passing through and had nothing to do with the bank robbery. He emphatically stated that he knew nothing about it. The more Sam listened the more he felt he recognized the softness in the man's voice. He sensed that the man was filled with love and could never be a bank robber. The man was questioned over and over again and even threatened with harm if he didn't give the information they wanted.

Sam continued to listen to the conversation and learned that the man's name was Samuel. He didn't learn much more than that. They all got off at the same station. The deputies escorted the man in the direction of the local jailhouse. Sam arrived home, put everything away and went to the magazine to drop off his pictures and stories. The publisher was happy to see him and told him that after all this time, they better be good. Sam assured him they were and that he was going to take a few weeks off to rest. Sam told him he was expecting an old friend to show up in town and wanted to spend some time with him. The publisher agreed and said if he needed him, he would call.

Sam walked down the street trying to think of what he could do to help the man on the train. As a reporter, he could come and go almost anywhere without being questioned. He decided to visit the jailhouse and ask if there was anything going on that might make a good story. The sheriff, who enjoyed publicity and was always willing to talk to the press, welcomed him with open arms. He was just beginning to talk about himself when one of the deputies brought the man through the office area to fingerprint him.

Just as they came into the room, Sam rushed to his side, grabbed his hand and said, "Samuel, what took you so long? I thought you would be here hours ago! It really is great to see you! How are Mary and the kids?"

The man was in shock and couldn't say a thing. Sam was glad that he couldn't. The sheriff walked over and said, "Sam, you know this man?"

"Know him? Why we've been friends for over twenty years or so. I've been waiting for Samuel. He is supposed to be staying with me for a week or two while his wife is out of the country. Samuel, how did you know to find me at the jailhouse?"

The man just stood with his mouth open. The sheriff was beside himself and told the deputies they had made some kind of mistake. He ordered them to let this man go to be with his friend. The sheriff then told Sam to please come back later and he would have something for him.

Sam went out the front door of the jailhouse with Samuel under his arm as if trying to hurry him along before the sheriff changed his mind. They made their way to the local restaurant and sat in a booth where they could have a cup of coffee and not be overheard by other customers. Samuel sat silently while Sam ordered something to eat and drink. When the waiter left, Sam explained why he did what he did. He asked if Samuel would confide in him to see if he could help him. Sam took some time to tell about Matt and their adventures with Hank and some of the other strangers from a hidden city. Samuel's eyes grew large as he listened with great excitement. When Sam paused, Samuel took a minute and properly introduced himself. He assured Sam that he was from that very same place, but never knew where or how to begin the journey back home. He went on to say that he has never crossed paths with any of the others that had disappeared. He felt they must have all just vanished in the water. The water was the last thing that he could remember; everything was dark after that.

They ate and hurried back to Sam's place where Sam introduced Samuel to Moses. Samuel shook Moses' paw and said, "Hello boy. I feel like I already know you."

Samuel then sat down at the table with Sam and started making plans for the two of them to make two journeys. One would be to Matt's place, the other to Samuel's home. Sam explained as much as he could about what they would encounter on their trip to the hidden city. Then, he purchased some new supplies for their trip. He also stopped at the magazine office to pick up another assignment. Two weeks later, they were on a train and heading for Matt's place with great excitement.

They arrived in town just before sunset. In the general store, Sam was told that there was a man looking for him a few days earlier. The man had been sent to Matt's place. The store clerk didn't know if he was still around because no one had seen him since. Sam and Samuel bought a few items and then headed for the trail to Matt's cabin. Before long, they were in sight of the cabin and the excitement of being back was overwhelming. Quickshaw was flying in overhead as if to greet Sam and Moses and meet the new guest.

When they arrived at the edge of Matt's front yard, they could hear a yell from a window where the curtain had been pulled back. Matt had looked out just in time to see them approaching and he screamed with joy. He came running out of the cabin, down across the front yard and grabbed Sam in a hug that nearly crushed his ribs. Matt then knelt and did the same to Moses. Sam asked Matt to calm down long enough for him to introduce Samuel. Matt told them both he had quite a surprise for them and led them into the house. He kept talking and letting them know how much they had been missed. The feelings were mutual. Inside the house, there were three other men. When they saw Samuel, it seemed as though all heaven was going to break loose. The men and Samuel cried with joy and embraced each other for what seemed like hours. While they were having their reunion, Matt took Sam outside and gave him an update on what had happened during the time he was gone.

He said, "The three men had heard the story that we may have had something to do with some men who had disappeared. They decided to come to talk to us."

Matt also told Sam that he and Quickshaw had been to seven graveyards to check the names on the headstones. "Any names I found that had no relatives, I sent back to the hidden city via Quickshaw. The replies were that all of them, except for one, had come from the hidden city."

"I guess we now know what happened to all the male adults from the hidden city, Matt. Too bad we hadn't been around to help more of them to return." Sam said as he tried to smile again. "Now, at least we can help Samuel and the others."

The next morning some men from town, who had been out hunting the day before, were on their way back to town. They stopped at Matt's for a quick drink of cool water. They noticed that Sam had returned. They also saw the four strangers but made no comments. Although they noticed that Matt and his guests were preparing for another one of his hikes, they did not ask any questions. They had their water and just continued on their way. Moses followed the men as if he wanted to make sure they kept going. They stopped just at the edge of the trees and knelt as if looking back to see what, if anything was happening. Moses ran closer to them and started barking wildly as if he were going to attack if they didn't keep going. The men rose to their feet and started moving quickly in the direction of town. Moses returned to Matt's cabin and took his place next to Sam. Sam patted him on the head and told him he was a good dog. The packing was completed and the plans were made for the hike to begin early the next morning.

A hardy breakfast was on the grill. As the sun appeared in the sky, the sheriff was standing at the edge of the clearing. He stepped close enough to ask who each person was, where they were from and how long they expected to be gone. As they answered him, he wrote it all down. "Expect to see you fellows in town or on your way out of town when you get back." he jested.

Sam broke in and tried to tell the sheriff that the men were going to go their own way once out in the wilderness and didn't expect to come back through here. The sheriff just looked at Sam and told him that he knew of no other way out of there. He then gave him a look as if he thought they were up to something they didn't want him to know. The sheriff just looked at all four men. He told them to be careful and keep an eye out. He hoped to see them when they got back. Then he helped himself to a cup of hot coffee, grabbed his rifle and headed down the path toward town.

Breakfast was finished and the long journey began again. The weather was perfect and the temperature was the just right for hiking. Because a couple of the men were not used to hiking the way Matt was, they had to plan on having more frequent breaks. This meant that they would be moving at a slower pace than Matt and Sam had become accustomed to. The journey would take a little longer. Sam took a picture of the men while Matt made a note to tell the people in the hidden city that they were coming. Matt then attached the note and pictures to Quickshaw and sent him on his way.

After two days, Quickshaw returned and had a note attached for Matt. Matt removed the note and quickly took Sam aside to share the contents. There was a concern that all these men were not from the hidden city. One of the men who claimed to be Josh Becket had the right name but the picture was not of Josh Becket. Matt and Sam had to come up with a plan. He wondered why the others did not know that Josh Becket was a fake.

That night, after supper, Sam took Samuel off by himself to a quiet stream just below where they were camping. Moses tagged along with them. Sam shared the letter with Samuel. Samuel's reply was that he wouldn't have known Josh because they were of different ages and had different tasks in the city. He may have seen him there but not enough to know what he would look like so many years later.

The other men were taken one by one. One went with Sam, another with Matt. Then they had to figure out what to do about Josh. None of the men could be sure it was him for one reason or another. The question remained. *What was Josh doing here and how much did he know?* Matt finally took him away from the others by telling him they needed to do some scouting of the trail. While they were gone, Sam went through Josh's belongings. There he found a book written by Josh Becket, *"The Gold Left Behind in the Hidden City"*. Sam also found some local newspaper clippings of men who went on hikes with Matt and Sam into the wilderness but never came back. In the bags, Sam found identification that identified this 'Josh Becket' as Thomas Lawson. Sam realized that Josh Becket, the writer, must be the real person who should be going back. This new 'Josh' must be in search of the gold he thinks is hidden somewhere in the hidden city. Everything was put back as it was. When Matt and 'Josh' returned, Sam asked Matt for a minute of his time and told him what he had learned. One at a time, again, the men were taken off and a plan was devised to get them back to the hidden city, but to have 'Josh' find himself in a completely different area.

Quickshaw was sent back and forth with messages between the two camps to let them know what was happening. As they came into the first group of caves that was still two days away from the hidden city, the plan began to unfold. 'Josh' was the first to be taken to a cave with Sam and Moses while Matt took the others toward the hidden city. There was more than enough to keep 'Josh' looking with Sam. Before they knew it, Matt returned looking for them and asking if they had seen the others. Sam was delighted that the plan worked so well. 'Josh' was fit to be tied because he felt they were pulling something over on him. He insisted that they knew where the city was and demanded that they take him there.

The next morning at breakfast, they told him they knew who he was and that he was on a wild goose chase. There was no gold in the hidden city, at least not the kind he was hoping to find. He became very upset and threatened to go off on his own, because it must be close by. They took time to tell him of some of the things he might come up against. He decided that he would return with them, get his own scout, make his own journey and keep all the gold for himself. They all agreed that they would make the trip back as soon as possible. Moses was growling and keeping an eye on 'Josh' as if he didn't trust him either. When they were packed and ready to go, Moses stayed close by as they headed down the path.

'Josh' was not very good company on the way back. All he did was murmur and complain. Matt and Sam did their best to ignore him. Once in a while, they would try to lend some words to discourage him from going back to seek out the hidden city. He said that no matter what they told him, he was bound and determined to find the city and get the gold he had read about in Josh's book. Matt and Sam were only thinking about how they would try to find the real Josh and bring him back to his people, if that was what he wanted. The journey back was a long one. Finally, they were at Matt's cabin and 'Josh' was on his way down the path to town.

Days passed by as Matt and Sam made plans to get to the city to try to locate the real Josh and explain to him all that had happened. It took them two weeks, but they finally located him. He was living in a small cottage at the edge of some woods overlooking a beautiful valley just at the foot of the mountains. Josh greeted them with open arms and was very excited as they told their story to him. As beautiful as this place was, it was not home. They helped Josh pack what he wanted to take with him. They decided to leave bright and early the next morning. Moses was also glad they were going back to the wilderness of Matt's cabin. He loved it there and could be content there forever. They left on schedule at five in the morning. The train ride back was uneventful. Matt, Sam and Josh got to know and respect each other very much. Josh had never dreamed he would ever find his homeland again. He was very grateful to both of them.

Josh had a lot of questions so the trip back to Matt's cabin went by pretty quickly. It wasn't long before they arrived at the station in town and were on the loading dock gathering up Josh's belongings. They stopped by the general store to get something cold to drink for the hike home. As they entered the store, a lot of men in the town were jesting and making fun. Sam and Matt told Josh not to pay any attention to them because they meant no harm. The store owner did say something about his loss to Matt and how sorry he was about the cabin. Matt just pushed it off as another little remark and went about his business. He threw the money that he owed on the counter and turned to Sam and Josh and said, "Let's get going. This place makes me sick!"

The three of them went down the road and were happy to be so near. Moses ran ahead and was greeted by Quickshaw at the foot of the path that led up to the cabin. Soon the cabin was in sight, or at least what was left of it. While they were away, the cabin had burned to the ground. All that was left was the fireplace chimney. There was nothing now except an area covered by debris where the cabin once stood and the yard had been.

"*What a mess! How could this have happened?*" Matt repeated, over and over again. Moses walked to the back corner of where the cabin once stood and quickly came back with a fairly new gasoline can squeezed in the teeth of his mouth. He brought it to Matt. The can looked like it may have come from the local store. Matt checked it. He was able to see enough to tell him that it did come from Mike Potter's general store in town. Sam couldn't find the words to tell Matt how sorry he was about his loss. He assured him they would help him rebuild even better than it was. He said no one was leaving until Matt's cabin was standing and the yard was cleaned up. Matt very softly said, "Thank you." Then, with the gas can tightly gripped in his fist and with Moses walking behind at his heels, Matt headed toward the path that led back to town. Soon he was out of sight. The other two set up camp and made a fire to prepare the evening meal.

Meanwhile, Matt made his way back to the general store. He was met by Mike Potter with a shot gun in his hands. The sheriff and two deputies were standing by his side. They started by telling Matt they wanted no trouble. They said that the person suspected of having done it had disappeared with three others in the wilderness just north of the cabin. The sheriff said that he, with his deputies and some of the townspeople, tried tracking them to bring them back to justice, but had lost their tracks. He said there was no trace of them after a heavy evening rain storm. Matt listened, but said nothing. Surprisingly, some of the townspeople offered to come up and assist in rebuilding Matt's cabin when he was ready. Matt just listened. He was too upset to say anything.

Matt returned to have his supper with Sam and Josh. He told both of them the story the sheriff had given him. After supper, the three of them started cleaning and piling up the debris to burn what was left. Moses also helped out by dragging what he could to the pile. Matt finally took a break and went to sit on an old stump to the side of where they had built the campfire. Quickshaw was soon at Matt's side as if trying to comfort him. Matt fed Quickshaw some crackers and bread and patted him on the head as if to tell him everything was alright and that he would be okay. The evening was clear, silent and as beautiful as ever when Matt laid his head down that night. The three men talked about rising early and made a plan for the next day's work. They would start by clearing the rest of the debris and getting everything that had burned out of the way. Then they would prepare the floor plan for the new cabin.

They awoke early and worked on a list of supplies they would need to get started. Just as Matt was ready to head to town, a group of about eight townspeople were on their way up the path. Included in the group was Mike Potter, the general store owner. They were coming with many of the supplies that Matt had planned on purchasing today. Mike yelled ahead and said, "I hope there is plenty of hot coffee in the pot! That's quite a hike up here, especially when you're carrying all theses supplies. So where do we start?"

Matt wasn't sure if he was happy or sad, but did his best to shake his hand and greet him with a smile. The work began and before the sun set, the frame was up and the floor was down. Some ladies, girls and a young boy showed up with some food for the evening meal. They cooked it while the men were finishing up for the day. Then they served it as the men moaned and groaned about their aching muscles after working so hard all day. Matt ate nothing. He just sat alone in the middle of the framed cabin on a sawhorse. The room would later be the kitchen, living and dining area. Matt sat there noticing how empty it all looked. All his carvings and homemade furniture were lost forever, just like the family he had lost many years ago. He sat there with tiny tears falling to the floor below him. The others respected his need for privacy.

The next day the building continued. This time, the cabin would have two separate bedrooms with bunk beds. This seemed like a good idea considering all the company Matt was having recently. It took exactly one week to the day for the crew to rebuild the cabin and have Matt ready to move into his new home. Many of the townspeople brought Matt things that they could spare and Matt might need. The house didn't have much. To Matt, it all seemed like a bad dream and an answer to a prayer at the same time.

Matt asked everyone to gather at the front steps of his new porch. Although he had a difficult time finding the right words, he did thank them all for what they had done. From that day forward, Matt and the townspeople had a whole different relationship. Many people in town offered to watch over things if Matt were to let them know when he was leaving. Matt in turn told them, that anyone looking for a good guide into the wilderness, that he was their man, at no charge. Matt took Sam aside and told him because of all that was happening that day, maybe it was as close as they would come to the life in the hidden city, but they both agreed it was a start in the right direction.

# Chapter 5

# The Last Trip to the Hidden City

Now that everything was back to normal, it was time to make plans to get Josh back to his people and the place he missed and loved so much. Josh tried many times to get Matt and Sam to make the hidden city their home. He thought they could just stay there away from the 'rat race' of this life. Although Matt and Sam were tempted, they decided they were content where they were for the time being. They felt they had other commitments. They also valued each other's friendship and were pleased to have found some new friends in town.

Moses and Quickshaw were awake first and waiting in the yard for everyone to start the trip and get moving. They began to make a lot of noise. Apparently they were trying to wake the rest of them to let them know they were losing a lot of good daylight. It was usually a good idea to get going while it was cool and the sun wasn't too bright.

Before long, they all were going in the direction of the hidden city. They talked about how exciting it was to be going back once again. They all agreed that they were seeing many beautiful sights along the way, but none of them could compare to the beauty hidden within and behind the walls of the hidden city.

One night, as they sat quietly around a flickering campfire, Sam said, "You know, Josh, after I saw your beautiful hidden city, I chose not to take any pictures or write about it. I was afraid someone would discover and destroy the beauty and peace everyone enjoys there. I'm so curious. What made you write about it? Come to think of it, I don't even know if your city has a name."

Josh, with a big smile on his face explained, "I wrote the book for two reasons. The first is that I like to eat." He paused to see if Sam or Matt would laugh. They gave him a little smile.

Josh continued, "The profits from the book provided money for food and a place to live. There weren't many jobs available for a stranger at the time. I thought whoever read my book would just find it interesting and think it was fictitious. I really doubted that anyone would believe it was about a real place."

Sam could tell that Josh honestly didn't think it was as big a deal, as he knew it was.

"The second reason was that I had hoped if there were others out there that had survived as I did, they might look me up and together we could search for our homeland. I was fortunate enough to sell a lot of books, but I never heard from anyone who claimed to be from my city. I did hear from one man. He wanted to know if the city did exist and if it was really filled with gold as I said in my book. I never heard from that man again so I figured that was the last time I ever would."

Matt explained that, that must have been the man who claimed to be Josh in the last group of men going to seek out the hidden city.

Later, Josh told them the name for the hidden city. He said "It is simply called, *"The Haven of Rest"*. We've always called it that as long as I can remember." All agreed that it was certainly that, and the name was very appropriate.

Quickshaw was called and sent off with a message to the *Haven of Rest* to let them know that they were on their way and should be there in the next couple of days. All was going well and the friendship between the three men was getting stronger everyday.

Quickshaw returned the next day around breakfast time. Matt had just removed the note from Quickshaw's leg when four men with guns burst into the campsite telling them all to raise their hands over their heads. One of the men was good old Thomas Lawson, the man who had claimed to be Josh. He was also one of the men the sheriff suspected of burning down Matt's cabin. Thomas had denied everything with a smile on his face saying he had nothing to do with it, while the other men just laughed.

Matt, Sam and Josh were quickly tied up. All they could do was watch as the male intruders enjoyed their breakfast. Unfortunately, the men also found the note that Quickshaw had brought from the hidden city. In all the excitement, Matt had dropped it. The four men were insisting that they be led to the city or they would kill their captives, one at a time, in front of the others. Sam and Josh were amazed when Matt so quickly agreed to lead them. Once breakfast was done and everything had been packed, they were well on their way. They traveled in and out of caves, up and down paths, along narrow paths and through heavy forest. Finally, they were in the cave where Moses was stranded. This is when Sam realized that Matt had a plan to deal with these guys. Once he knew that, Sam became much more quarrelsome with Matt to make certain the men would think he was still very upset with Matt's decision to help them. The men told Sam to shut up and stay out of it. They pushed him back into a dark corner of the cave. As Sam fell back on his side he felt something furry with teeth nipping at his hands. At first he was scared to death, but then he quickly realized it was Moses. In moments, Moses had bitten through the ropes and Sam's hands were free. Sam stayed still for a few more minutes waiting for just the right time. Matt pointed out the vine and explained to the men about the opening of the rock door on the other side of the narrow gulley. One of them quickly grabbed the vine and as soon as he put his weight on it, the rock moved just as Matt said it would. The first man crossed and sent the vine back for the second man. The second man was well on his way across and yelling to Matt. "So long sucker."

He instructed the others to throw Matt, Sam and Josh into the narrow gulley so they would never be heard from again.

Just about that time, Sam made his decision and leaped to his feet. When Matt saw him coming, he jumped into action. They each took one of the men and pushed them into the narrow gulley. Now the vine was returning to their side of the gulley. Josh wasted no time grabbing it and holding it loosely. One of the men fired a shot back at them just as Josh let enough pressure off the vine to allow it to close again tightly, securing the men inside as it did with Moses.

Sam, Matt, Josh and Moses made their way to the giant waterfall and got everything ready to go to the underwater cave and into the berry patch cave on the other side. While they reviewed with Josh what they had to do, he suddenly realized what had happened to him years ago. It seemed strange now that he was never able to remember how to get back here. It all seemed so simple. He must have been in shock and stumbled, like the others, until someone found him in the woods and took him to safety.

They were in the water and, in minutes, made their way to the berry patch. They settled in for a good night's sleep. They awoke early to wait for the sun to shine on the cave door and create the opening to the hidden city. This time, unlike the others, the whole city was there to meet them. It was a glorious day! Sam and Matt, once again, were treated with a hero's welcome. Everyone was so excited that Josh had been found and safely returned home. He was the last of the lost taking into consideration those that Matt had discovered were buried in the world on the other side.

Sam, Matt and Moses spent the next three days at the village. They were joined by Quickshaw on the second day. The days were filled with a lot of celebrating and getting re-acquainted. Grandfathers, uncles, sons and brothers, who had all been given up for dead many years ago, were finally being reunited. The villagers never expected to see them again and they never expected to be back in the village they loved so much. While there, many of the villagers tried to encourage Matt and Sam to stay and make their home with all of them. Matt and Sam were tempted to take them up on their wonderful offer, however they both had things they still wanted to do. They also told them that for now they, too, were content where they were. The next morning, they left the village with many mixed emotions. As they told everyone goodbye, they felt that this might have been their last visit.

The sun had now opened the door to the berry patch cave. Once again, they were on their way back home. Soon they were at the waterfall and unpacking their things for the long journey homeward. They approached the cave where the two men had been sealed behind the moving stone on the other side of the narrow gulley. Now, they had to make a decision as to what to do with them. They decided they must give them the opportunity to toss away their guns and surrender. Matt slid back into a dark part of the cave and Sam gently put just enough pressure on the vine to open it. Sam, at the top, was able to be in the dark out of sight. The men appeared to be fine. They were told to toss their weapons into the narrow gulley. Then they would be helped back to the other side where Sam and Matt were waiting. The plan worked as Matt said it would. The men tossed their weapons into the gulley and were soon back with Matt and Sam. As they came across one at a time, they were tied up with the very ropes that they used on Matt, Sam and Josh. They asked about Josh and were told that he had gone home and they would never see him again. In the next few days, Sam and Matt were able to get them all back to a familiar area. They offered to let the men go if they would leave the hills and never return. In exchange, Matt and Sam would give them just enough supplies and food to get them out of there. They promised, if given the chance after all they had done, they would leave and never return. As they left, Matt told them to make sure they kept their end of the bargain or the next time they would be dealing with the sheriff. The men, disappointed, dejected and defeated headed out to make their way home. They went down their path and were soon out of sight. Matt and Sam were glad to be rid of them. They headed down their own path toward home.

After a couple of days, they were in sight of the new cabin. They couldn't wait to get a good night's rest. When they arrived at the front door, they found someone had left them a copy of the magazine that had Sam's article and pictures in it. There were many beautiful, breathtaking pictures including a picture of Matt with Quickshaw on his shoulder.

Matt had not realized Sam had taken such a picture. Sam had given Matt all the credit for the wonderful pictures and for the content of the article. He felt that without his help, it would never have been done so well or finished to the extent that it was. As Matt and Sam looked at the pictures, they had a good hardy laugh. Then they showed them to Moses who barked as if he, too, was having a good laugh. They enjoyed being home again. They were able to sleep on real beds with the fire flickering and crackling throughout the night.

## Chapter 6

# A Surprise for Matt

The following morning, Sam and Matt awoke to a beautiful sunrise. They enjoyed a hardy breakfast at fireside in the front yard. They spent the day splitting wood for the fireplace and stacking it near the cabin. They cleaned out the old shed and weeded the overgrown garden. Later, they made their way into town to visit the people who had been kind enough to help rebuild the cabin and clean up the fire debris.

They arrived home pretty late that evening and found the sheriff and two of his deputies sitting on the front porch waiting for them. As they approached, the sheriff asked where their new friend Josh was. They explained that Josh had gone home and would probably never return.

The sheriff gave them an "I'll bet" look and said, "I just want to warn you to be on the lookout for the men who, I believe, burned down your cabin. They are still on the loose." Then he and his deputies left on the path toward town. Before going out of sight, he turned, waved his hand and yelled, "Good luck."

Matt and Sam were ready to call it a day when they heard shots coming from the direction the sheriff and deputies had been heading. They slid on their boots and grabbed a pistol. They headed down the path as fast as they could. They made their way quickly, but quietly, along the path. Suddenly they heard voices. Looking through some trees, they could see some men in a clearing just off to the right. They positioned themselves behind some big trees where they wouldn't be seen. They could see that the sheriff was holding his shoulder as if he had been wounded. One of the deputies was lying on the ground and the other was looking over him as if he were dead. Matt and Sam could see now that it was the same two men they had released back at the hidden city. It looked as if they had jumped the sheriff and his deputies by surprise, taken their guns and shot them.

Sam and Matt were able to get closer to each other and discuss how they were going to handle the situation. They each agreed on which of the two men they would take. Suddenly, shots rang out sending both men to the ground. The sheriff and the deputy had managed to grab the guns. The other men fell to their knees and finally to their bellies. Neither was hit very badly; each just had arm wounds. The sheriff had a pretty bad shoulder wound and the deputy's appeared to be more serious. The two men were cuffed. Sam and Matt were able to make a stretcher and roll the wounded deputy on it. They all made their way back to Matt's cabin except the deputy who was not shot. He was sent back to town for the doctor and some other help.

By the time the doctor arrived, Matt had the sheriff's wounds cleaned and bandaged pretty well. The deputy had been cleaned, also and was ready for the doctor. He was in a lot of pain, but the doctor, after examining him, said he was in no danger of dying. He patched him up and asked Matt if he could stay there for a couple of days to get his strength back. Naturally, Matt agreed and the deputy was given complete rest for the next couple of days. A few of the men who came back from town with the deputy were sworn in as new deputies. Now they could assist the sheriff and bring the prisoners back to town. The two criminals were sent to the state capitol to be tried for all their crimes. Matt and Sam were called in to testify. The two men tried to tell their story of the hidden city. No one believed them. The sheriff supported Matt and Sam as they told the judge about how these men had ambushed them, once, also. The two men were found guilty on many counts and sentenced to twenty years each with no possibility of parole.

Matt and Sam decided to stay a few days at the state capitol to enjoy some of the historical sites. They also wanted to do some other sightseeing while they were there. Although they found everything to be very interesting, they were glad to be going home in a couple of days.

The wounded deputy had recovered and gone back to town while Sam and Matt were still at the state capitol.

Sam and Matt had a fairly quiet journey on the train going home. However, when they arrived at the station, the whole town was there to greet them. They had planned a big celebration for Matt and Sam because they considered them to be heroes. Neither Matt nor Sam wanted to be a part of it. They did not refuse, however, because they appreciated all the hard work the townspeople had done preparing for it. The celebration lasted all day long. Sam and Matt enjoyed the day and all the delicious food. At the end of all the celebration, the town gave Matt and Sam a thank you plaque for their act of bravery. Finally, the celebrating was over and they made their way to the path and headed home.

For the next few days, Sam worked on his new article for the magazine and planned on leaving by the end of the week. The week went by too quickly for both of them. Sam and Moses were once again on the path to town and quickly out of sight. Quickshaw flew in to spend some time with Matt as if he sensed that Matt was going to be extra lonely in the days ahead. As the days passed, Matt had only the company of Quickshaw and a couple of passing deer. He made a few new wooden stools for the front yard and soon became extremely restless.

Matt decided to use his time re-carving the figures of his wife and children, and the one of Sam and Moses he had lost in the house. When completed he thought to himself, 'they were even better than before'. Because Matt had a lot of time to himself now he decided to make a carving of Quickshaw, which he had never done before. He even took the time to carve one more of the Big Black Bear, and beside him, his family. His last carving was that of the beautiful waterfall from the inside of the cave, with the pond at its base. He was even able to create the fountain of water in the center of the pond that rose even higher up than the height of the waterfall itself.

He felt he needed to get away for a while. Matt closed everything up, and with Quickshaw flying high above, headed off in a direction he had never been before. He was gone for three weeks before feeling the need to go back home. He came across a lot of interesting sights that he knew, in the near future, he would like to share with Sam and his camera. There were some flowers and rock formations that Matt had never seen. He was sure Sam's readers would enjoy looking at pictures of them, too. He had to admit he really missed Sam and Moses. It wasn't the same without them around. He wondered how they were doing as he hiked along the long rocky pathways. He thought he would drop them a line when he got home to see if they were up to taking another hike anytime soon. Maybe he could even talk Sam into a trip to visit with their friends at the hidden city, *The Haven of Rest*.

Matt and Quickshaw spent a lot of time just wandering wherever their feelings lead them. Matt would stop and camp by a clear sparkling lake and swim out and just lay on his back looking at all the splendor about him. He often would lay quietly on a hillside very still so he could watch the many different animals search for food and play in the free wilderness, where man seldom came. There was a peace that Matt had experienced that few would ever experience in their lifetime. Matt and Quickshaw shared many a meal and many a campfire together, and Matt almost hated to head back to his cabin, but he knew it was time.

As they headed back to the cabin, they would take turns catching fish for their meals. Quickshaw would often times spend time in the air putting on a show of very skillful flying for Matt. Matt in return would skip along, or roll down a hillside, and do flips in the air as he jumped over a mound of dirt here and there. They were finally getting close to the cabin now.

As he came in view of the cabin, he could see smoke coming from the fireplace chimney. He was very excited because he figured it could not be anyone else but Sam and Moses. He began walking at a much faster pace, almost jogging. As he came in clear view, he could see it was Sam and Moses. Moses came running at such a fast pace that he couldn't slow down. He almost knocked Matt to his feet. Matt got to his knees, gave

Moses a hug and told him he was very glad to see him. Matt and Sam were very excited to see each other again. They had so much to say that they kept interrupting each other until they finally just stood back and took a moment to catch their breath and start over again. Sam finally stopped and asked Matt to sit awhile and just have a quick talk. Matt had never seen such a serious face on Sam. This was a side of Sam he never saw before and he was a little concerned.

"What's wrong, Sam?"

Just as Sam was about to explain, a young man's voice could be heard yelling for Moses. Moses' perked up his ears and went running toward the cabin.

"Who's that?" Asked Matt as he looked over Sam's shoulder to see a young man in the yard still calling for Moses.

"That's what I have been trying to tell you. That's your son!"

"My, my what? How? How? Where? Where? How can it be?" Matt murmured with heavy tears in his eyes. "It can't be!" screamed Matt. "He died with my wife and daughter in the flood—in the flood many years ago."

On the way down the path to the yard, Sam was trying to get Matt to take some long deep breaths and relax. Just as they came to the edge of the yard, a young lady and a woman came through the front door and stood there on the steps. They looked as if they were seeing a ghost. The woman collapsed and fell to the ground. The girl went quickly to her aid. Matt and Sam rushed to lift her and bring her into the house. They gently put her on the bed. The woman was unconscious for hours. During that time, the girl and the young man talked with Matt, their father. Sam stayed with Matt's wife until she recovered. Then he helped her into the kitchen and living area where Matt had just finished making some juice for everyone to drink. When Matt and his wife were face to face again, they both just looked at each other as if they had been rejoined by death itself. After a long period of staring in silence, they were in each other's arms with tears flowing down their faces. Sam took the children outside to give Matt and his wife a few minutes to themselves.

Soon, they were all together again in the front yard. Moses was jumping up and licking Matt's face with great joy. They all had a lot of questions. They wanted to know everything the other had been doing all these years. Sam had started a campfire outside and had made some chili and biscuits for supper. Quickshaw flew in to see what all the excitement was and was introduced to the long lost family. After the meal was over, Matt took his wife off the stool and went off for a walk, they didn't return for a couple of hours. While they were gone, Sam shared many stories about Matt with the children. He told them about how he and Matt had met and the incidents with the big black bear. He finished by showing them the plaques that the town had recently given them for their bravery.

They could not believe that they spent all these years thinking the others were dead and would never be seen again. That night they all slept under a star filled sky. When morning came, they were joined again by Matt's faithful companion Quickshaw. Everyone fell in love with Moses and Quickshaw. They enjoyed spending time patting them and feeding them. Ethan, Matt's son, was overwhelmed by the animals and quickly built a close relationship with both of them. It was as if they had known each other forever.

The next few days were just spent talking to one another and getting to know each other better. Melinda Megan was a senior in high school and Ethan was in junior high school. Ethan was playing baseball and doing very well. He played first base and also did some pitching. Melinda belonged to the drama club and had been in many plays at the school and local town events. Matt could see how proud his wife was of both of them. She beamed as she spoke about each of them and what they were doing.

Matt's wife, Meredith, had a job in the finance department of a very large insurance company and was doing very well.

Now, it was time for them to leave. Meredith had to go back to work and the children had to go back to school. Their time together had gone by too quickly. Everyone was hoping this moment would never come. However, now they had some difficult decisions to make. This was going to be quite a change for all of them because, at this point, their worlds were so very far apart. It was an easy decision according to Matt's wife.

"We have everything we need in the city. We are all set and very well organized. You cannot expect us to sacrifice all that for this wilderness where we would have absolutely nothing. Why, Matt, you don't even have a job!" A hurt and worried look came over Matt's face.

Meredith continued, "I think it would be best if we all move back to town and live in the city. We can use your camp, as just that, a camp, a place to go on vacations."

It all made sense to everyone except Matt. He looked at Sam and asked him to take a walk with him. He wanted to discuss his point of view to see if there might be another way. As they walked Matt began verbalizing some of the thoughts going through his head. "What would I do in the city? Where would Quickshaw be? What about all the things I love and enjoy here in this beautiful wilderness?"

Sam just listened to his friend. Then they began reminiscing about all they had done and the places they had gone over the years. Sam did not try to influence Matt's decision one way or the other. He knew this was something that only Matt could decide. If this is what Matt wanted and if he was ready and able to make such a drastic change in his life, Sam would support his decision. Matt had the chance to have the family he lost so many, many years ago. Matt had to decide which meant more to him, his family or this life of freedom.

While Matt and Sam were out walking, Meredith and the children had packed everything. They were ready to go to the train station the first thing in the morning and be home late the following evening.

When Matt and Sam returned, Matt explained to his family that he wasn't sure he could live in the city. The family also agreed that they knew there was no way that they could live here in the wilderness. They could not give up their friends and the life to which they had become accustomed. They took time to try to explain how much easier everything was for them in the city. They had all the comforts life had to offer. They did not have to go very far for anything. Sam was amazed. After all these lonely years of being separated by a tragedy and enduring an emptiness that couldn't be satisfied. Matt and his family were having a difficult time trying to decide how and what to sacrifice so that they could all be together again.

It was also time for Sam and Moses to leave. That was never easy because they loved it out here as much as Matt did. Sam wondered where they were going to go if Matt moved back to the city.

The time for departure arrived. The decision had been made. Everyone was going to live as they had been living. Sam agreed to see that the family reached the train station safely. He was going that way, anyway. With tear filled eyes and many apologies, the family departed. Matt stood on the front porch and watched as they disappeared out of sight, down the path to town. Suddenly, Matt was filled with a great emptiness. He forgot about his many reasons for staying and grabbed a bag. He threw a few items in it and went running down the path. He caught up with them in a matter of minutes and told them that he was sorry that he had been so selfish. All he wanted was to have them all together again. There were many more tears and hugs. Sam followed behind them and watched them as they headed toward the station as the family unit they once were. He could hear them continually saying "I love you" to each other.

Matt found the trip to the city, where his family was living, was very long and quite uncomfortable. Sam had to get off at the second stop. Before Sam left, Matt promised to write as soon as he was settled. He said that he would like to set up a time for a visit in the near future.

Finally, they arrived home and everyone, except Matt, was very excited. They had a tiny three bedroom house squeezed in a small housing development with a little yard that had fake plants and water fountains. There was nothing wrong with the house. All the furniture was fairly new and there was carpeting on the floor. Although it was all clean and neat, Matt was having difficulty trying to understand how he could live there. He vowed to himself that he was going to give it his best for the family. He already missed Quickshaw and wondered how he was doing. He wondered if Quickshaw felt that Matt had just gone off and abandoned him.

Before long, all the neighbors came by to say hello and meet the long lost man of the family. The children's friends came by also and Matt felt them looking at him as though they had never seen anyone like him before. Then some of Meredith's friends from work stopped by to say hello and welcome him home. They all crowded around the house to welcome everyone home, and let them know they were glad they got home safely. Some of them came out of curiosity, to meet the long lost father of the wilderness they had read about in Sam's magazine article. Matt felt extremely uncomfortable. He thought he was being examined and laughed at because of his speech, mannerisms and clothing. Matt tried to be patient with them and everyone did their best to be polite and sociable. Matt disappeared into the house to catch his breath and wondered what he was doing there.

As he leaned up against the kitchen stove, his wife appeared, "Matt, you can't just walk away from people. That's very rude! What do you think my friends are going to say if you walk away every time they pay a visit?" Matt caught his breath, took her arm and went back to the gathering with her so as not to cause any more trouble. This was going to be harder than Matt had thought.

Soon, the yard was clear of everyone except for the family. They all worked together getting things put away. Then, they got ready for bed. Tomorrow was going to be a busy day just trying to get back to normal. Matt and his wife sat up a little late and talked about Matt's getting a job. However, there would be no rush. His wife thought that he should just take a week to get settled in and get used to being in the city. They would look at the want ads and see what Matt would like to do when his wife returned from work in the evening.

The next morning, everyone was up and getting ready for school or work. Matt could not believe how hectic a scene it was. There was no time for the family to sit down for breakfast together. Each of them just grabbed a piece of toast or an English muffin and swallowed some milk or juice. They said "I love you" to each other and rushed out the door. Matt stood there in awe as he watched the beginning of their day. All too soon the house was empty and quiet. He just stood there for a moment and tried to figure out what had just happened. If this was the beginning of the day, he couldn't imagine what the end of the day would be. He took the time to get dressed, picked up, washed and put away the dishes. Then he straightened up the house a little before going outside and having a better look at it in the daylight. As he looked around, he didn't think it looked any better than it did the night before. The first thing he did was pull out all the fake flowers and anything else that he thought was a waste.

He continued trying to fix the yard to make it look better. He heard a woman's voice call to him, "What are you doing?"

He introduced himself and shook the hand of what turned out to be one of the neighbors. The neighbor began explaining to him, "You must know that Meredith has spent a lot of time and money on everything in this yard. You might want to check with her before changing anything. Besides" she added "everyone in the neighborhood feels that it looks nice just the way it is." Then she gave him a funny look and walked toward her own home.

Matt continued working in the yard. Every once in a while he would sit back and think about Quickshaw and his beautiful cabin in the wilderness. It was a very long and lonely day for Matt. He was really looking forward to having his family home that evening. Ethan and two of his friends arrived home first. He quickly introduced them to Matt and asked him to visit with them while he got his baseball equipment. Soon he was back out with a pastry in his hand and rushing down the street yelling back, "Tell Mom I'll be home right after practice and pizza with the guys." He and his friends were soon out of sight.

Melinda Megan was the next to arrive home. She also had her friends with her. She made some quick introductions and told her father that she had to hurry back to school to rehearse for an upcoming play. She had her visit with him while she was going around the house and getting what she needed. She then rushed off with a piece of pastry in her hand and yelling, "Tell Mom I'll be home as soon as I can, but don't wait up."

It was already late when Meredith finally arrived home. It was well after what Matt thought should have been supper time. When she walked in the door, she gave Matt a quick kiss on the cheek with and said, "I love you. I missed you today." Then she mumbled something about what he did to the yard. She hurried into the bedroom and then to the bathroom. When she came back to the kitchen, she was all dressed as if she were going to a party. She looked at Matt and told him she was sorry, but she had to meet a client tonight and would probably not be home until late. She told him that he should fix himself something to eat and not wait up; because it might be too late by the time she came home. Then she, too, was off in a flash.

Matt was alone again just as he had been all day long. It looked like he was going to be alone all night, too. He sat on the front porch with a sandwich and a glass of juice and thought to himself, *What in the world is going on? Is it like this every day around here?*

Matt had read a few magazines and was sitting at the kitchen table when Ethan arrived home. Ethan told Matt about his practice and a little bit about the pizza shop. Then he said he was tired and had to get some sleep. He kissed his father goodnight and told him he loved him. When Melinda Megan arrived an hour later, she did and said the same things before going right to bed. By the time Meredith came home, Matt was fast asleep on the couch. She just left him there.

The following days were the same, day after day. Matt felt invisible. It was as if he wasn't even there. He certainly didn't feel needed at all. Friday night finally came and Meredith and Matt had a chance to look at the newspaper ads to see what Matt could do for work. Matt tried to talk to her about the busy life style she and the children had, but she just smiled and said, "Isn't it great? There is so much to do. It's not like where you were where you have to go looking for something to do."

Matt tried to listen to her and calmly share that he was feeling this life reminded him of a big rat race. He said there was no time for each other or for the family to do anything together. Then he asked, "How will they ever find time to go to the camp?"

She just looked at him and told him he was again beginning to get selfish. She said, "You ought to sell that camp, anyway. None of us really wanted to go back there anyhow. I'm sure we could find good use for the money. For instance, we could add on a sun room or have more money to spend on the children. There are a few things, I could use, too."

Matt was getting frustrated. He walked out the front door and down the street to find a place where he could think more clearly. His head was still spinning with all sorts of problems and questions. "How could I ever even think of selling the cabin or not going back?" The thought of never seeing Quickshaw again was too much for him to fathom. He sat on a park bench and his eyes were filled with tears. A man approached him and asked, "Are you alright? Is they anything I can do to help?"

Matt thanked him for his kindness and told him everything was fine; he just needed some time alone. The man handed him a card and went on his way. A short while later, Matt looked at the card. It was from a local minister at one of the area churches. Matt put the card back in his pocket and headed back to the house.

When Matt arrived home, everyone was there. Matt's children were there laughing and eating popcorn with their friends. Matt asked them if he might have a few minutes with them out on the porch. The children excused themselves and told their friends they would only be a minute or two. Meredith walked out with them. They let Matt know, again, that it was very rude of Matt to ask them to leave the room, especially since they had guests. They wondered why the discussion couldn't have waited until they left or even until tomorrow.

Matt just looked at them with tears in his eyes and asked, "How do I fit in this family? How do I fit into your world? I love you all and want us all be together, but we never are. Please tell me what I am supposed to do?"

Matt's wife broke in, "Matt, as soon as you get a job and some friends of your own, you'll be fine. You just need to get going."

The children all agreed that when Matt got his own job, his own friends and his own entertainment, things would be looking brighter for him. They said that his problem was that he had too much time on his hands. They all smiled and said they would spend sometime with him tomorrow for a couple of hours. They could look through the want ads with him and find him a place to work. Then they returned to their friends and continued the evening without including him. Matt went to bed. He stayed awake wondering how he could make sense of this new life. Then he sorted out his options. Maybe a job might help. Maybe, somehow, he could get involved with Ethan's baseball. Maybe he could go to Melinda Megan's rehearsals. He thought and thought until he finally fell asleep.

Saturday came and nothing changed. Right away, friends were there to get each member of the family started on some type of activity, none of which included Matt. They all said they would look through the want ads with him later. They never got around to it. On Sunday, the family all went to the first service so they could get church out of the way as early as possible. They already had their plans for the day. They looked like the ideal, happy family on their way to and from church. After church, however, everyone was scurrying around to begin their own planned activities. Matt's wife also had planned her afternoon months in advance with some of her female friends. Husbands were not included. Plus the girls wanted to know more about, how it was living with a real wilderness man

Matt returned to the church and found the minister in the backyard with his family. When the minister saw him, he invited Matt to join them for some juice. The minister introduced his family and they all spent the afternoon together. Matt shared his story with them and asked if they had any advice to offer. They agreed with Sam that it was certainly a difficult situation. Perhaps the minister could start by trying to get Matt and his family to visit them together to see if they could just sit and listen to the feelings and concerns of the other. Matt and the minister agreed that there seemed to be the common bond of love. That was the best place to start as far as they were concerned. The minister was able to set up a meeting for all of them to meet next Thursday evening at seven o'clock.

In the meantime, Matt got a job and his employer and co-workers loved him. He was working for a local nursery with plants, flowers, trees, shrubs, fertilizers, plant foods and anything that had to do with enhancing nature itself. Although Matt loved his job, he felt tied down and still didn't feel like part of the family he loved and wanted so much.

The meeting was set and everyone attended. Before they started, Meredith made it clear that she only had one hour to spend on something she felt was not needed anyway. They all had many things to say, but at the end, Meredith insisted that the problem was that Matt needed his own friends, his own hobbies and his own entertainment. Then he would be fine and the family would get along quite well. As they left for home, the minister patted Matt on the shoulder and told him he'd be there if he needed him. The two men seemed to have a great respect for each other.

The following evening, Matt and the minister went to a local fishing hole where they spent a few more hours getting to know each other. Matt offered to have the minister and his family visit the camp when Matt took his first vacation. The minister said that if he and his wife could manage the time, they would love to take him up on his offer.

Matt knew there was no way he was ever going to sell the property that he worked so hard to get and so long to build. It also held great memories of Sam and Moses and the kind townspeople who helped him rebuild.

As the months passed by, the only thing that kept Matt going was the thought of that first vacation and a visit to the camp. Plans were made and the family agreed to go even though they were not too excited about spending any more time there. They wished Matt could see how disruptive it was going to be for them to have to go there on vacation. Matt had suggested that they take a friend along and do some camping, real camping in a tent or cave or whatever. They all explained that their friends weren't really into that. The minister's family, however, was very excited about joining Matt's family for a vacation at the camp. They could hardly wait for the experience. Finally, the time came and Matt was busy packing for the trip to be taken the next day. He had it all planned and had written to Sam to join them. They would leave on the early morning train, meet Sam on it and be at the camp by mid evening. Matt was so excited, he had all he could do to wait for morning. He had a difficult time trying to sleep that night. In fact, he didn't get much sleep. When he did get up and was ready to go, he was told by his wife that, late last night, the rest of the family had decided not to go. They didn't want to upset him and didn't want to face him, either. Matt's wife tried to talk him into putting his stuff away. She said the family could do something else at another time. Matt had nothing to say. He just headed out the front door and down the street to the train station with his camping gear.

When he arrived at the train station, he met the minister and his family who were still very excited about going. They were all saddened when they heard the news about Matt's family deciding to stay home. They boarded the train, right on schedule at five forty five. The children were asking Matt all kinds of questions about the camp and Quickshaw. They couldn't wait to meet him.

Soon, they were at the stop where Sam and Moses were going to join them. It was a fantastic reunion! Matt introduced them to the minister and his family. Now they were on the last leg of the journey to the camp. On the way, Matt filled Sam in with all that had happened. The children played the whole time with Moses. Sam was saddened by the story Matt shared with him. He told Matt that he was going to try and prepare him for the life he was headed into; however felt Matt had to experience it on his own. He told Matt that he knew he would be fine, because of the love he had for his family.

Sam and Matt talked for a while about how Quickshaw might be dealing with all this, and how much they had both missed him. Sam was telling Matt that Moses really perked up when he was told about going back to see Matt and Quickshaw. Sam spent some time talking to the Minster and his wife and showing them some of the pictures he had taken during his visits with Matt. They had told Sam they had read many of his articles, but never thought they would be going to where the pictures were actually taken.

Sam went on and on about many of the adventures he and Matt had been through and the many different people they had met along the way. He told about the time Matt's cabin was burnt to the ground. About the time the tree had fallen on Matt's leg. He told about how they met in the beginning and how Matt saved them from the Big Black Bear. How they had later saved the bears life and how the Big Black Bear had come to their aid many times after that. As Sam told the tales to the minister and his wife the children's eyes grew wider and wider. They were soon at their destination.

# Chapter 7

# The Long Awaited Vacation

The train arrived right on schedule. The station manager remembered Matt and Sam and welcomed them. They went through town and stopped at the general store to pick up some supplies. Mike Potter was there and told them he was glad to see them again. He told Matt many of them had gone by the camp to keep an eye on it. Everything was just as it was when he left. Matt introduced everyone and Mike asked about Matt's family. Matt told him they were fine and it was a long story that he would share with him when they all had more time. Matt hadn't been this happy in months. He couldn't wait to lay his eyes on the cabin and Quickshaw again.

Soon, they were ready to begin their walk on the path to the cabin. It was a long hard journey for the minister and his family because they were not used to this type of hiking. Even though Matt was excited and in a hurry, he slowed the pace down to make it easier for them. It wasn't long before they were near the cabin and they heard a screech from above. Down came Quickshaw and landed right on Matt's right arm. The minister's children, Andy and Mary, were so excited. After all they had heard about Quickshaw, they were finally going to meet him. Matt reached into his pocket and handed them some crackers so they could feed them to Quickshaw. Neither child had ever experienced anything like this. You could see by the smiles on their faces that it was just the beginning of a very exciting week for them.

The cabin was now in sight and the two children ran ahead running in circles of joy and freedom. It was as if the city never existed and they had been freed from a life that had kept a fence around them. Soon they were all on the front porch. Their eyes grew as they entered the cabin that was filled with coziness, peace and just the feeling that there was finally a place where you could kick off your shoes and relax. Matt and Sam went around and opened the windows. They assigned the back bedroom to the minister and his family. From that bedroom, you could hear the nearby brook running all night. It was also on the side of the cabin where the sun rose in the morning.

Sam had the children gather wood for the outside campfire. Tonight, he and Matt were going to make everyone a home cooked meal on a campfire. This was something none of them had ever had. As the children gathered wood, Moses was close behind them and he, too, brought some wood back that he clinched in his teeth. Soon, the meal was ready and everyone was sitting around thoroughly enjoying it. They all said that they had never really tasted food as good as this. Quickshaw had spent mealtime with them and now was ready to return to his home high on the side of a cliff, not too far away. Sam and Matt told the children that they would hike to Quickshaw's home tomorrow where you could see the many wondrous beauties of the wilderness for miles and miles.

The rest of the afternoon was spent getting everyone settled and preparing a plan on how they were going to spend the week. They all knew the week was going to go by very quickly. When night came, everyone was in bed except for Matt who went to his favorite stump near the campfire. He sat down slowly with tears in his eyes. Moses was soon by his side and was pawing his right arm as if to tell him everything was going to be okay.

A few minutes later, Sam came to his friend's side and asked if it would be alright to join him. Matt wiped the tears from his eyes and used the excuse that he was perspiring from the warm weather. Then he told Sam he would be more than happy to have him join him. Matt took a minute to tell Sam just how much he had missed him. The two men talked of their trips together, especially of times they visited the hidden city. Both agreed that it was a shame that the whole world couldn't be like that wonderful place. Matt began to share with Sam what had been happening with his family. He was puzzled about what was going to become of them as a whole. Sam wished he could tell Matt that he believed everything would work out and they would one day be a happy family again, but he could not. He really didn't believe it himself. He admitted that he really didn't know what to tell Matt or what kind of advice to give him. The two men just sat there, talked and wept until close to three in the morning when suddenly little Andy, the minister's son, appeared at their side. Matt was the first to notice him and asked, "What in the world are you doing up at this hour young fellow?"

The young man looked at both of them and just said, "How do you sleep in all this peace and quiet?"

Both Sam and Matt changed their tears to laughter for the next moment. Sam took a minute to explain that he, too, had a hard time adjusting when he first came to the wilderness. However, as he listened, really listened, to the sounds of the night, they became like a giant orchestra playing soft music and filling the night with a song that Sam named, *"Sweet Dreams."*

Matt took young Andy in his arms and sat him on his lap. He began telling Andy of way back when he first came here. He said he often was scared to death by the night sounds, but he, too, like Sam, came to realize they truly are the most wonderful sounds. Matt said it is unfortunate that most of the world will never hear them and what a shame that is. As Matt continued to talk, Andy fell sound asleep on his shoulder. Matt carried him back to the cabin where he put him on a blanket on the floor in front of the fireplace next to where Moses slept. The two of them slept soundly for the rest of the night as did Matt and Sam once they, too, had turned in.

The morning sun rose with such beauty that the minister and his wife just sat quietly in the rocking chairs on the front porch as if they had died and gone to Heaven. Before long, the aroma of fresh ground, fresh cooked coffee was in the air and the bacon and eggs were crackling in a frying pan over the outside campfire. As they ate, the minister and his wife couldn't thank Matt enough for inviting them. They could not believe that Matt's wife and family did not mind missing all this. Matt made excuses for them and said he understood that this was a different way of life for them. He said maybe someday they could all return together.

The minister was truly overwhelmed about the peace and the joy he found while here and commented, "Wouldn't it be wonderful if it were like this everyday?"

Matt almost tripped up by beginning to tell him that there was such a place where life was like this everyday. Sam interrupted him and quickly tried to change the subject. The minister looked at the two of them as if they were trying to hide or cover up something that they wanted to keep hidden. Soon they were all busy talking about a short hike Matt had planned for late morning. They only had to get a few things ready because they were just going to be gone for a couple of hours. They would be back well before night fall. The children were so excited and they were ready in five minutes.

Soon, they were on a trail heading north of Matt's cabin. They were out of sight of the cabin. Remembering that the minister and his family were not used to hiking, Matt and Sam tried to keep a slower pace for them so they wouldn't get tried or discouraged. Every once in awhile, Sam would find a spot where he could see what would make a great photo. Often, he would take pictures of the entire family with Matt, then with himself and many of just the children and Moses. He was able to take one of them when Quickshaw flew in and sat on a tree limb just next to the children and Moses. It was almost as if Quickshaw didn't want to be left out of the pictures.

When afternoon came, Matt picked a place he had been before to make camp. There was a beautiful pond with a brook flowing into it from high above. He told the children if they were to climb to the top, the brook would slide them right into the pond. He walked to the top with them the first time just to make sure they got there safely. The minister and his wife also decided to wade in the pond once they saw the fun the children were having. Moses followed them to the top and he also took a turn at letting the stream slide him down into the pond. Lunch was ready and the children couldn't stop talking about how much fun they were having. They wished they could live there forever. All the adults looked at each other in great silence for a moment because they were thinking the same thing.

Before long, when they were back on the trail again, Matt motioned to them to stop and be quiet. Then he walked ahead and down into some trees. Soon he was back and motioned for them to continue to be quiet, but to follow closely behind him. Then he had them all kneel. He pushed back the branches of a nearby bush very carefully and quietly. Then he pointed to where they could see a very large mother bear washing her cubs in the stream below. The cubs did not appear to be enjoying the bath. The minister's children could relate to that and giggled silently with their little hands over their mouths. It was quite a sight, sitting there and watching as the cubs came out and shook to get the water off their bodies. Mother bear stayed in the water just long enough to flip a fish to each of them from the stream as if rewarding them for being good during bath time. They watched for a little bit longer and then mother and her cubs headed into the woods on the other side of the stream.

Everyone was back on the path in seconds asking all kinds of questions about the different types of berries and plant life they saw as they walked along the beautiful path. Many of the berries were good to eat and they were able to try some. Matt explained that many of the berries were too deadly to consume by themselves. However, when they were mixed together they made some much needed medicines. Matt took time to show them many things they could do to survive if they were ever stranded in the wilderness. He took time to show them where to find or build a safe shelter. He explained so many things. He told and showed them different ways of building a fire, things they could dig out of the ground for food and how to elude animals that might be dangerous. He even told them how, on a very cold night when he first came to the wilderness, he dug a hole and buried himself to keep warm. Matt had all kinds of stories and the children couldn't get enough of them. In fact, Mary always carried a small notebook with her. She took as many notes as she could about the stories Matt told. Sometimes she was not sure if Matt was stretching the truth just to make the tale bigger than it really was. Somehow, she instinctively knew Matt would not do that.

Before they knew it, it was time to turn back so they could make the cabin before nightfall. Everyone was a little sad because it had been such a wonderful day and they hated to have it end. However, they had to admit that all this new and exciting way of life made them pretty tired. They looked forward to a good night's sleep. They sang many songs on the way back that Matt had made up since he came to the wilderness. He claimed that because he had such a bad singing voice, the wild animals wouldn't come near him. They had to stop to rest twice on the way back. When they arrived at the front yard, the sun had just about set.

No one, including Sam and Matt, was hungry so they called it an early night and headed off to bed. As they expected, they all slept like logs that night and had a lot to talk about the next morning. Because Matt had not been at the cabin for some time, he wanted to visit a few old friends near town. He told everyone this would be a day that they could do something they wanted to do by themselves or they were welcome to join him. Seeing how much he wanted to visit and catch up with his neighbors, they decided to stay and spend some time by themselves.

The minister and his wife did some of the laundry and hung it out to dry on Matt's clotheslines. Andy and Moses headed down the path as if going to town. Andy's mother reminded them not to go too far. Mary took her notebook and found a quiet place where she could be alone to rewrite her notes and make some additions.

It was the beginning of another beautiful day. At lunchtime, they all gathered together for cold drinks and sandwiches. Matt was still in town. Once lunch was over, the minister and his wife decided to take a nap. Andy, Sam and Moses grabbed the fishing poles and went off to try to catch some fresh fish for supper. Mary went back to her notebook and was having a great time just updating and re-reading her notes. The minister and his wife were taking the clothes off the line and folding them to put them away.

About five o'clock in the afternoon, Matt was making his way back into the front yard. Sam and Andy were coming through the opening with an armful of fish for the evening meal. The minister and his wife were glad to see them all returning and suddenly realized that Mary was not back yet. Mary had neglected to tell anyone where she was going, so no one knew where to find her. They wanted to let her know that it would soon be supper time. The minister and his wife started supper and the rest went off hollering for Mary as they walked.

An hour had passed before they were all back at the cabin and still no sign of Mary. Now everyone was getting worried that something might have happened to her. Matt instructed Sam to go off to town to see if anyone would help in the search. The minister's wife would remain at the cabin in case Mary returned. She was taught how to fire a pistol. She was told to fire two shots twice if Mary returned to let the rest know she had been found. No one returned to the cabin until it was too dark to see what they were doing. They asked Matt what the next plan was. There were now twenty of them looking for Mary and no one had a clue where to start.

The Minster and his wife were assured by Matt that Mary would be found safe and sound. The minister led all the searchers in a moment of prayer and then Matt asked them all to go home for the night. Once everyone had gone off to bed, Matt asked Sam to keep the campfire burning while he made one last attempt, with a torch, to find Mary. He was out of sight quickly and into the woods behind the house. Matt did not know where to go or where to look. He took a moment and asked God to help him stumble across the place where Mary was, good or bad. He walked for hours. As the sun rose, he put out the torch. He found a big rock nearby and sat down to take a rest and catch his breath. As he sat there, he thought he could hear what sounded like someone crying. He turned and went quickly in the direction of the sounds. There, before him, he saw Mary buried up to her head in the ground. Matt quickly uncovered her, wiped her tears and asked what had happened. She admitted that she had gone too far and couldn't find her was back. She had remembered what he said in one of his stories about burying himself when he was cold. She said she did it because she was scared.

Matt took his pistol and fired two shots two different times hoping they would hear it back at the cabin and know Mary was okay. Then, he helped her brush off all the dirt as best as he could. He took her hand and headed back in the direction of the cabin. It was noon before they finally got there. No one had heard the shots so the new search parties were all searching again. While mother took Mary to get her cleaned up, Matt fired the shots again and soon everyone was back at the cabin and glad to join in for an early afternoon lunch. Everyone agreed that there was always something exciting happening when Matt was back in town. They all had a good laugh.

The week was coming to an end faster than they had expected. With all the excitement, the week just seemed to disappear. It was time to pack up for the return trip home. The only happiness was the fact that they had been able to come and experience such a life. The cabin was closed up once again and they were all heading down the path to town. Soon they were at the train station and everyone was very silent. Matt was off to the side by himself and writing. When Matt heard the train pull in and the announcement that it was time to board, he placed what he was writing in two separate envelopes. Everyone's baggage was on the train, except for Matt's. The train was ready to leave. Matt pulled the minister aside and told him he wasn't going back just yet. He handed the two envelopes to the minister and asked that he give one to his wife and family and the other to the place where he worked. The minister said he would be glad to do it and hoped everything would work out for the best. He thanked Matt for the greatest week of their lives and asked if they might return again should time allow. Matt told him that his home would always be open to him and his family. The two men embraced and the minister jumped on the train as it was leaving the station.

Matt turned to get his baggage and when he did, he saw Sam standing there with Moses. The two of them just smiled at each other and embraced. Matt could feel Sam's hand patting him on the back. They stopped by the general store for something cold to drink and then headed up the path to Matt's cabin. The train pulled out of sight and so did Matt, Sam and Moses, with Quickshaw flying high above. Sam could not leave this time either. He finally realized his place was here with Matt and he to sent a letter to the publisher to let him know, if he still had a job, he'd be working from here.

Sam, Matt and Moses made their way back up the path out of town and with sounds of laughter and singing they could be heard yelling. "It's good to be home! It's good to be home!" Moses was barking as if singing alone and Quickshaw was screeching high above as if he were joining in. A new beginning in the wilderness for Matt and Sam was now about to begin.

I knew not what I missed, until I realized what I had. I had become complacent, and then willing to set aside my values for the things I grew to desire. The things I saw drew me further away from the things I loved. It was hard to go back, but go back I did, and here I'll stay.

# Sam, Moses, Matt and Quickshaw

Through the hills together they traveled and walked
Of its splendid beauty they always talked
Sam, Moses, Matt and Quickshaw
Were always amazed at the things they saw

They met face to face the big black bear
And then with him life they did share
The trees, the sky and a rainbow in awe
Matt would be dead if not for big bear's paw

The trails went down, but many were steep
Great joy from great beauty they'd often weep
They were always there if one had a need
They shared all they had; they had no greed

They shared and cared and were almost like one
In each and everything they did, it ended up as fun
They laughed, they cried, comforted each other, too
They not always agreed, but disagreements were few

They took no trips, nor hiked without first a plan
Reviewed it and made sure all would understand
Where to stop for water, camp or take along
Always something to read or to sing a campfire song

A rainbow like never had been seen, nor ever will
Was seen this very day, from high on the hill
From the damp darkness to the entrance of a cave
Light came forth from the sun the rays it gave

When life is as it should be and you're with your best friend
When troubles come your way on him you can depend
You have no empty moment nor pain so deep it cannot heal
When deep in suffering together you both will feel

There are no overwhelming burdens anything to face so great
For he'll always be there and you'll know that he's your mate
So thank the good Lord for all the beauty here and there
For everyone, one and all, and always show that you care

My companion, my friend, my love, my wife
I have found you and now have found my life
Let us now together become as one
And in all we do together, we'll have fun

978-0-595-41605-9
0-595-41605-5

Printed in the United States
76373LV00005B/364-378